BEINGS

Brandon Eldridge

To mom and dad, with love.
Thank you for everything.

CONTENTS

Chapter 1 1

Chapter 2 7

Chapter 3 11

Chapter 4 19

Chapter 5 25

Chapter 6 28

Chapter 7 33

Chapter 8 40

Chapter 9 42

Chapter 10 48

Chapter 11 51

Chapter 12 52

Chapter 13 53

Chapter 14 57

Chapter 15 62

Chapter 16 66

Chapter 17 73

Chapter 18 78

Chapter 19 86

Chapter 20 93

Chapter 21 100

Chapter 22 109

Chapter 23 116

Chapter 24 122

Chapter 25 128

Chapter 26 132

Chapter 27 135

Chapter 28 143

Chapter 29 150

Chapter 30 154

Chapter 31 159

Chapter 32 166

Chapter 33 170

Chapter 34 176

Chapter 35 181

Chapter 36 185

Chapter 37 190

Chapter 38 193

Chapter 39 198

Chapter 40 200

Chapter 41 205

Chapter 42 209

Chapter 43 212

Chapter 44 217

Chapter 45 222

Chapter 46 226

Chapter 47 232

CHAPTER 1

The monsters under our beds don't exist in the daylight. The eyes glowing in the closet seem to disappear with the sunrise. During the day, nothing can get us. But at night? At night, everything changes. Trees look less like trees and more like living creatures. The night is terrifying.

It was 2:30 am when he sat straight up in bed from a deep sleep. Covered in sweat, he wasn't sure if he had heard a noise or if it had been a dream. Either way, something told him to get up (*now!*) and look out his bedroom window. Garrett Bradley peeked through his blinds wearing nothing but his blue pajama pants. He saw what he expected to see; the dark of night, the moonlight hitting his wooden privacy fence, and a branch from the tulip tree that had made its way into the front of the bedroom window. He had been meaning to trim that.

Calming down, assuring himself that the noise he had heard was a dream, he relaxed and gathered his thoughts. A loud crack came from outside, as the wind blew the branch that needed trimming across his window and into the vinyl siding. The rough edges of the branch made a screeching sound against the vinyl. Garrett jumped, instinctively putting his hands up to his face. He laughed as he rubbed his face and hair. "I need a guard dog," he said to no one.

He jerked awake when the alarm clock on his phone buzzed. 6:15 am, Friday, July 29th. It was supposed to be a soothing, calming alarm, but what alarm clock was soothing at that hour?

There's no such thing.

It was the type of morning where he was in disbelief that it was time to start the day, questioning the passage of time. He rolled over onto his right side to silence his phone and check if he had missed any calls or messages throughout the night. As usual, there was nothing but a few emails. He lazily placed the phone back on the nightstand and rolled over.

The sunlight had just made its way through his bathroom skylight, forming a ring of light in his bathtub. The light showed streaks of soap residue around the tub; if Garrett had noticed it this morning, it would have driven him crazy. His obsessive-compulsive disorder would have made him clean it before he could even leave the house.

He could tell today was going to be another scorcher. July in Michigan (and throughout the Midwest) can be almost unbearable, today being no exception to that rule.

After rubbing his eyes and stretching out across the entirety of his bed, his feet finally touched the floor as he let out a loud yawn. The carpet, cool and soft, felt good on his bare feet. He glanced up at the standing mirror on the other wall, noticing the left side of his hair sticking straight up where he had been lying on it.

His mornings were usually the same mundane routine. His alarm clock went off at 6:15 every morning during the work week. Then he'd half stumble out of bed and head to the bathroom to relieve himself. Sometimes he would throw on his red and blue plaid robe, and sometimes he'd stay in pajama pants that did the trick just fine, then he'd head to the kitchen for breakfast. *The best meal of the day*, he'd tell himself.

He started the coffeepot and made his cup of coffee, which was always the same; one lump of sugar and two teaspoons of milk, never understanding how someone could drink their coffee straight black. He had tried it once when his grandpa had offered him a sip. The bitter taste never left him, staying in his mind like a sweet memory. The memory would pop in, now and then, whether he wanted it to or not, making him miss his grandpa all over again.

He grabbed a bowl from the cabinet, then the box of cereal from the top of the refrigerator. He yawned again.

The refrigerator shook as he opened the door, the inside light hitting him like a freight train, making him squint.

As he ate, the morning sun was coming in through the kitchen window like an angelic beam, warming the perfect rectangle it made on the floor. He scrolled through his email, swiping his thumb upward on his phone. He had a local grocery store coupon offer and a message from a coworker about a spreadsheet that needed to be checked before submitting to his supervisor. He figured that one could wait until he walked into work in about an hour and a half. He sipped his coffee, thankful it was Friday.

Just get through today.

Garrett Bradley was an IT guru and had loved technology his whole life. Now twenty-seven, he had graduated from the University of Michigan, receiving his bachelor's degree in Computer Engineering. He then attended the Ross School of Business and received his MBA. To say he was intelligent would be an understatement. He graduated summa cum laude in both undergrad and grad school.

Immediately after grad school, he took a position as an Information Security Engineer with BelTech, one of the biggest computer engineering firms in all of central Michigan. Only three years into the job, he had made his way to Senior Lead of his department. He had everything an organization could want; the brains, the looks, he never called in sick, and was never late. Garrett Bradley stood out to everyone he met.

He hopped out of the shower and folded the towel around him- his final task before throwing on clothes to complete his routine. Today's attire was typical; a red polo shirt, khaki pants, and his favorite red tennis shoes. He grabbed his laptop case with all his essentials in it, clipped his name tag and ID badge onto the left pocket of his tan khaki pants, and headed out the door. There seems to be more pep to one's step on the last day of the work week. Garrett welcomed the pep, noticing he had it today.

It instantly struck him how hot it already was this early in the morning. He squinted and let out a "*whew*," knowing the day would be like the inside of an oven. As usual, Mr. and Mrs. Klein, his retired next-door neighbors, were sitting on the porch enjoying each other's company, the way retired married couples do.

Mr. Klein yelled over to Garrett, "Gonna be a hot one today," he said, taking another sip of coffee.

"It already is, Mr. Klein. Makes me wish I would have had a pool installed this summer," Garrett shot back.

Mr. Klein smiled in agreement.

Mr. and Mrs. Klein, who had lived on this cul-de-sac for thirty-five years, both waved as Garrett got into his black Toyota Camry he had just purchased the summer before. Garrett longed for a marriage like theirs one day. An image of a wedding day yet to happen played out in his mind like a silent movie. It made him smile.

Black cars make the hot days seem even hotter, and Garrett instantly felt the heat as he sat in the driver's seat and started the ignition. The leather squeaked as he adjusted in the seat. He looked in the rearview mirror one last time and checked his hair, then made sure he didn't have anything in his teeth. He had brushed his teeth that morning, but he was obsessive about keeping them pristine. He even kept a travel toothbrush and toothpaste in a drawer in his desk at work.

He flipped on the air conditioner, the hot air hitting him like a blowtorch. He put on his black sunglasses and backed out of his driveway. Even with a rearview camera, he still turned around to check behind him. The gravel in the road crunched under one-year-old tires that had been foam cleaned just two days ago. He gently put his foot on the brake and put the car into drive, beginning his twenty-minute commute to the office.

"Today will be a good day," he said to himself as he adjusted his sunglasses. He had a great feeling and was in a great mood. He was completely unaware the invasion had already started.

CHAPTER 2

Forty-five minutes north of Garrett's front door was a three hundred and seventeen- acre farm belonging to George Ehren. George had inherited this farm from his father, Stanley Ehren, when he had passed away from a heart attack at the age of fifty-five.

This farm, which was on a dirt road off of Route 9, had two beautiful barns, one red, the other brown and graying from years of sitting in the different midwestern seasons, freezing and thawing over and over. There was a large pond that sat in front of the wooded area on the east side of the property, big enough to pull out a small paddle boat or oar boat, which they never did. Instead, they'd fish from the dock or swim close to it. Occasionally, they'd float on a raft, but they'd rather swim or fish.

The farm was well secluded; you'd never know anyone lived back here if it weren't for the old white wooden mailbox that sat alone at the entrance of the dirt road. They preferred it that way.

If you were to drive down the dirt road, sending a screen of dirt flying behind you, you would see an ocean of corn and soybeans on your right-hand side. On the left was a row of trees that separated the Ehren farm from the Mitchell's property, the Mitchell's having moved there in 1986.

The dirt road wound around, eventually coming up to the white house that needed some updating on the right. It could use another coat of paint, and the doors and windows needed replacing badly. The roof, now eighteen years old, was splintered and discolored, and shingles hung loose and haphazardly.

The red barn sat adjacent to the house, the fields of corn and soybeans placed perfectly behind it, the scenery like something out of a Joan Miró painting. George's wife, Alexis, fell in love with the view of endless green the first time she saw it.

The pond had an old wooden dock Stanley Ehren had built in his younger years with his father, Lester Ehren—George's grandfather. Most summer days, after George's two boys had finished their morning farm-related duties, Tim and Jake Ehren would sit out on the dock, now knotted and rough with age, and fish until the day had become too hot.

Tim, who would be a senior in high school in the fall, usually gave up fishing much more quickly than his younger brother, Jake, who would be a freshman in a few months. This morning, as the sun peaked over the trees and heated the dock just enough to be bearable to sit on, Tim packed up his gear and headed for the house, leaving Jake to sit in the morning calmness alone. Jake preferred it this way, finding some of the joy in fishing being the quiet solitude.

Jake reeled in his line, checking to see if the worm was still on the hook. The line made a buzzing sound as it crept closer to him, his bobber dancing in the water from left to right, leaving a trail of bubbles and ripples in its path. He grabbed the line and held it up as the slimy worm hung there, dripping and lifeless from the rusty hook. He cast one more time, the hook and bobber making a splash that sounded louder than it should have in the quiet country morning.

Jake kicked off his sandals and placed them down on the dock neatly. He scratched a bug bite on the inner side of his foot, near his ankle. He leaned to his left on an old, splintered post that his grandfather had carefully built before he was a figment of his father's imagination. His eyes felt heavy, and he pulled his hat down toward his nose and covered his eyes. He started to drift off to sleep.

The line on his fishing pole made a click, and he raised his head. He didn't know if he had been asleep, but if he had, it had only felt like a minute. He reeled his line in once more, worried a fish had taken its meal and went on its way, leaving him with an empty, dangling hook.

He reeled and lifted the line. The cold worm hung there, sad and despondent. He cast again, sat back down, leaned against the old post, and yawned. He swatted at a bug that had flown past his face.

He shut his eyes, scratched his neck, and put his head back against the post, letting his feet dangle off the side of the dock, not quite touching the water. A refreshing breeze blew against his legs. A bubble from somewhere deep below emerged to the surface. The wind started to pick up, bringing in a sweet smell of corn. A second bubble, then another, rose to the surface and popped without a sound. A green hand slowly swirled under the water. From below the surface, yellow eyes looked up at the Michigan sky. The green hand broke the surface and guardedly reached for Jake's foot.

"Jake? Jake! Come on, I made some eggs and toast!" His mom said, then turned, going back inside the house.

The hand jerked back below the water, disappearing into its murkiness. Jake sat up, grabbed his fishing pole, and began to reel in his line.

The Ehren pond had been full of them for two days now.

CHAPTER 3

Garrett arrived at his parking space and parked as far away from the building entrance as he could, as he did every morning. He preferred to walk; he was in the best shape of his life. His brown hair sat perfectly combed over to the right and his facial hair was trimmed to a stubble, the length he liked to keep it. His eyes were a piercing green, as green as a freshly mowed lawn, and Garrett usually caught the eye of most women he passed by. He was handsome, coupled with the personality and brains to accompany those looks.

He had stayed single because his career was his priority, although recently, he had signed up for online dating, feeling more and more confident that he was ready to settle down and start a family. So far, he had had no luck on that scene, and was content with that fact. For now, he enjoyed his freedom. He had seen other friends not be able to meet him for golf or a day on the boat, and he was good, for now, having the luxury of being on his own schedule.

Garrett walked up to the front door of his office and held his ID badge up to the metallic door. The door made a clicking sound as the light turned from red to green, unlocking itself. He was glad it was Friday, and for a brief moment, he thought about the yard work he needed to do this coming weekend and, of course, about the Tigers game that was on that night. He looked forward to having a quiet night at home watching his beloved Tigers game, ordering a pizza, and having a few beers- a perfect example of the freedom he wasn't sure he was ready to give away.

He made the left turn down the long hallway that led past a series of offices and cubicles. He gave the famous midwestern nod to his coworkers and waved to Laura in HR. He had always thought she was beautiful, but she had always seemed a little too quiet for him. Regardless, he had heard of too many office romances going askew and would rather be no part of that statistic. Garrett Bradley, jumping headfirst into everything in life, except relationships.

"How do your boys blow a three-to-one lead in the ninth, Bradley?" His coworker, Dave, asked him as he got to his desk.

"Nothing surprises me anymore, Dave."

Dave Langley had worked at BelTech for four years longer than Garrett, but Garrett was Dave's superior on paper.

Garrett was also given more responsibility than Dave and earned more annually than Dave. Dave Langley was forty-three, had been divorced twice, and had two kids from his first marriage. He was a very easy-going guy, but he loved to give Garrett a hard time when it came to baseball. Growing up in Chicago, Dave was a true, die-hard Cubs fan. Their favorite baseball team is the only thing the two would ever disagree on in their day-to-day conversations.

Dave was going bald, wore black-rimmed glasses, and was extremely overweight. He would sweat working on a spreadsheet at his desk. He burped loudly, without regard to anyone in his vicinity. He had a small fan blowing on him at his desk all day, every day. Summer or winter, the buzz of the small, black fan could be heard over the clicks of his mouse and keyboard.

He was the total opposite of Garrett in every aspect, except for his love of baseball and technology. These similarities were enough to keep them at a place where they enjoyed working together, and they had formed a pretty strong bond and friendship in a relatively short time of working together. Garrett would tell you he could not ask for a better coworker, and Dave would say the same about Garrett.

Smiling, Dave said, "Don't let it get to you, Bradley. They have another chance tonight to do the same thing and rack up another loss." He was holding a plastic baseball, then threw it up in the air and caught it.

"Unfortunately, the way they are playing, you are probably right," Garrett said as he sat his laptop case on his desk. "I'm in a great mood today, and it's Friday," Garrett said to Dave as he raised his eyebrows. "Don't ruin it."

"Did you get the email I sent earlier? I just wanted to make sure the numbers are what you saw on your end," Dave said without looking up from his computer.

As Garrett was about to reply and tell him he had briefly skimmed through the spreadsheet, his front door alarm system dinged on his phone with an alert. Garrett ignored it, knowing every little thing trips the alarm. He had been meaning to adjust the sensitivity on the alarm last week when a leaf had floated across the lens and his alarm buzzed in the middle of a conference call.

He paused while the alert went off. He pushed the button on the side of his phone and turned the volume down. Garrett put the phone back in his pocket.

"A little. I will check it over after I update this security software Marcus sent over last night," Garrett said as he plugged in his laptop and logged on to the company's intranet.

"Appreciate 'ya," Dave said and took a swig of his coffee. The two remained quiet as they started their day in the world of IT security. The *tick* could be heard as Dave threw the ball in the air and caught it. He missed once, and the ball rolled to Garrett. Garrett picked it up, then tossed it back to Dave. Then silence.

Two hours had passed, time always seeming to move along quicker when there's work to be done, and Garrett stood up to stretch and refill the water bottle he kept at his desk. He had recently purchased a black canteen-style water bottle that he found kept his water ice-cold for practically his whole eight-hour shift.

As he walked down the hall, he again heard the front door alarm system's bell go off, the phone buzzing in his pocket. He frowned, trying to remember if he had any scheduled deliveries today. Confused but not paying any attention to his phone or the alarm system, he walked back to his desk, again doing the friendly nod to all of his coworkers. The water bottle dangled in his hand, swinging with each step he took. He saw a guy he worked closely with in another department on the phone. They both smiled and waved to each other. Garrett made his way back to his desk with about as much excitement as one has going to a dental appointment.

The workload Garrett had waiting for him today included searching the market for larger corporations who would be potential customers for security IT software, a task he didn't particularly enjoy doing. He started a new spreadsheet and took a drink of water.

Garrett rubbed the back of his neck and looked up at the clock. Another hour and a half had passed by, and hunger was starting to be a noticeable ache he could no longer ignore. A symphony of sounds growled in his stomach.

"I think I'm going to head down to Suzie's and grab some grub," he told his older colleague.

Suzie's was the company's café, located one floor down, which most of BelTech's employees called "the basement."

The food was on par with a high school cafeteria, which Garrett always thought was one step above hospital food.

"Enjoy," Dave said, uninterested, as they have had this exact same exchange what seemed like a million times. He raised a hand in a nonchalant wave.

Dave had not been down to Suzie's in over a year. He chose not to go down to the basement for a few reasons. The first being he packed his lunch every day. It usually consisted of some sort of lunch meat sandwich, a small bag of chips, a small bag of olives or carrots, and two "fun size" candy bars. The second reason was that it was expensive and snuck up on you if you weren't careful. He had a seventeen-year-old son who was about to attend college in the fall, and a fourteen-year-old daughter in high school. Dave had started saving up for their college, albeit a bit too late. His online poker habit, mixed with betting on sports, didn't help his situation.

Garrett sat down with his lunch of a large chef salad and an unsweet tea he had paid for with his badge. BelTech has a system that employees can pay for items at Suzie's and have it deducted from their paychecks. He mixed his salad and stared at the poster on the wall, which discussed the benefits of IT security and how BelTech is the industry leader in certain protective software, and as Garrett thought, "*blah, blah, blah.*"

He pulled his cell phone out of his pocket to check on sports and world news and scroll through social media. He couldn't deny it; he checked Laura's Instagram daily to see her latest pictures and to see if she was posing with any guys who could potentially be boyfriends. There were no new posts, and the relief made his shoulders relax.

Scrolling through the latest local news, he came across an article about an elderly couple who had been brutally murdered as they slept. What really bothered Garrett, though, was not how the couple had been murdered; it was how close the murder had taken place to his home. He lived in a subdivision on the west end of Burnley, Michigan, and this had taken place on the east side of Burnley, only about a ten-minute drive from his house. Those types of things always hit you a little differently when they are so close to home. He couldn't help but envision it in his head. *Were they aware of what was happening? Did they awaken to someone standing over them in their bedroom?* He had hoped not. The feeling made his stomach hurt as he took another drink of his tea.

The thought of what they had possibly gone through made him remember that his front door alarm system had gone off on his app a few times earlier that morning. Garrett swiped on his phone to find the app connected to his front door system. When the alarm is tripped, the camera records for up to three minutes, so you can see everything clearly recorded, in high definition. He had two recorded videos and was chewing on his salad when he watched the first. He waited through all three minutes. The video showed nothing on his front porch. His forehead wrinkled, and he watched again to see if he had missed anything. There was nothing on the screen. He decided it must have been the wind or an insect so small he couldn't see it. He swiped to the second video, noticing nothing on this one, thinking his system had gone a little haywire.

I'll check it out later, he thought to himself.

He thought about the elderly couple and how that same system might have given them enough of a warning to save them. Garrett finished his salad and wadded up his napkin and threw it in the plastic container, and stood up from his chair, ready to return to the world of IT Security. As he walked back to his cubicle, he searched for reviews online on his phone for customers complaining about receiving false alarms on their alarm systems. His front door alarm system was working perfectly fine. It wasn't a false alarm. It wasn't a false alarm at all.

CHAPTER 4

After Dave and Garrett had spent the rest of their Friday completing their menial day-to-day tasks, the two started to close down shop and get ready for their commutes home. Dave lived in an apartment complex, not even a ten-minute drive from the office.

Dave scratched his inner ear and said, "Big plans this weekend? I mean, besides watching your boys lose?" Garrett finished the last of his water and stood up.

"First of all, they aren't going to lose tonight. Second, I have a ton of yard work to do. I have some weeds to pull in the side yard. I'm thinking about putting some rocks down where some old mulch is to make it look a little better."

"I almost fell asleep listening to you tell me that, so I'm sure it'll be fun," Dave said as he was putting items in his bag.

Dave's weekends were usually less productive and uneventful; the kids would come over if they felt like it. He ate fast food or TV dinners for every meal and played online poker the rest of the time. He wasn't half-bad, either. Just last week, he made right under eight hundred bucks. He had nothing better to do.

Garrett told Dave goodbye and walked down the hallway out for Friday night's freedom. He wanted to wave to Laura and tell her to have a nice weekend, but she apparently had already left for the day. He would have to see her on social media.

Better than nothing.

He made it to the front door of his building, out into the heat, and noticed that the sky was a little darker now than he thought it had been when he had looked out the window, walking away from his desk. As he stood on the sidewalk by the front entrance, he looked up.

"*I didn't remember them calling for rain,*" he said out loud to no one.

He had secretly hoped it would rain because the yardwork wasn't exactly what he looked forward to in his free time, even though he knew it needed to be done.

As Garrett got into his Camry, he set his bag down in the passenger seat, exhaling as he got in on the driver's side. Every Friday night, he called his parents on his ride home. Jerry and Angela Bradley had been married for 30 years this past August. They had one child together, never having luck trying for a second. Garrett started the car, then spoke into his Camry's phone system to call his parents. He had just driven out of the parking lot when his dad, Jerry, picked up the phone and said hello.

"Hey, pops," Garrett said as he looked in his mirror to make sure he was clear to turn on the main road.

"Hey, boy," his dad shot back as he did every call.

Every conversation was virtually the same; they would discuss the week, the Tigers, what they were doing that weekend and, when Garrett's mom got her chance to speak, it was usually the same, followed by talks of any potential girlfriends. His parents couldn't tell over the phone, but Garrett was a little more distant tonight. He couldn't help but notice how the sky had become extremely dark in a short amount of time. He was amazed, noticing the slight green tint to the sky. It reminded him of a picture he had seen when he had contemplated visiting Alaska. He wondered if the northern lights looked anything like what he was witnessing now. The image popped into his brain momentarily, then left.

Garrett reached the entrance to his neighborhood as he was telling his parents goodbye on the phone. He rolled down his window and looked up to the sky as his car slowly came to a stop in the middle of the road. He could not believe how cool the day had become. In the Midwest, the weather can change in an instant. He pulled his cell phone out of his pocket to check the weather radar. He looked up at the sky again as his phone showed nothing on the radar. This made him disappointed, as he liked to pull up a chair, open the garage door and watch the storm make its way in. He felt like his dad when he did so.

"What in the world is going on?" he said as a slight breeze blew against his face. He got back into his car, put it into drive, and slowly drove toward the direction of home.

He pulled into his driveway, still studying the sky.

This is unusual. And why is there nothing on the radar?

He walked inside, put his keys and wallet on the table, then turned on the TV. The local meteorologists were as flabbergasted as everyone else, indicating no rain that evening and the weekend should be sunny and perfectly normal. The radar, which he would expect to show a conglomerate of green, yellow, orange and red, was as empty as his love life. He walked to his refrigerator, opened a beer, and changed the channel to catch the pre-game show.

He sat down on the couch, pulling out his phone to order pizza from his favorite local pizza place. According to Garrett, Valentino's had the absolute best pepperoni, onion, and banana pepper pizza you can find in the country. He ordered one with a side salad and sat back on the couch to catch the show.

Thirty minutes later, the doorbell rang, and his front door alarm system went off on his phone. He got up and opened the door to see the pizza delivery guy, an eighteen-year-old who looked half stoned, standing there. Garrett was too hungry to care. He noticed the sky was a little greener with a twinge of purple hue added since he last looked outside.

"What's the deal with this weather?" Garrett asked as he was handed the pizza.

"I don't know. There are a lot of tree branches down in the front of your neighborhood, too," the pizza guy said as he put his hands in his pockets. Garrett noticed the kid had a hard time maintaining eye contact.

"Really?" Garrett said, puzzled. "It doesn't even seem that windy."

"I know, it's weird, bro," the pizza guy said. He was more concerned with getting back to make another delivery than discussing the weather. Or maybe he was more concerned with getting back to his dope.

I'm too hungry to care.

Garrett sat through his game, which wasn't even close. The Tigers were struggling, never even scoring a run. He knew he would hear all about it from Dave on Monday morning.

Standing up, Garrett cleaned up his coffee table that had his pizza box, empty salad bowl, trash, and two empty beer bottles on it. He threw it away as he yawned, longing for a hot shower and to climb into bed, ready to put the work week behind him.

After what felt like one of the most refreshing showers of his life, he put on his blue pajama pants and climbed into bed. He thought about the yardwork he needed to do, and he dreaded it. He grabbed his phone from his nightstand and checked Laura's social media.

No posts. No boyfriend.

He pulled the blankets over him and rolled to his left side. A long yawn came out of him as he scratched his right arm. It took him less than four minutes to fall asleep.

Sleep is a funny thing. You lie there in an unconscious state, perhaps dreaming, perhaps not. You have no idea what's going on around you. You are completely unaware of your surroundings, just like Garrett, who, at this very moment, was being watched.

CHAPTER 5

The night was full of the typical summer sounds one hears in the Midwest. A bullfrog sang its song, seeming to call out to others to join in. Cicadas chirped and screeched, the high pitch buzz echoing off the pond. The wind blew a pleasant breeze across the Ehren farm.

The Ehren family slept in their beds, Alexis Ehren with one arm around her husband's waist. Down the hall, Tim and Jake slept in their bedrooms. Tim had fallen asleep clutching his phone. He had been texting a friend about a party happening in a few days, a party he would make sure his parents, devout Christians, would never find out about. Jake had fallen asleep reading the first book in a new series by his favorite author. The house was quiet and completely still. They slept, an occasional snore coming from George, oblivious of what was happening outside.

The Ehren's pond is where it started. It had been chosen carefully and tactfully. The first step for these creatures was to find a body of water surrounded by a lot of land. The Ehren farm had everything they needed. They could breathe underwater, which gave them an advantage during the day for hiding. They ate meat, so choosing a farm with access to all kinds of animals suited them perfectly, an endless supply, (for now) of pigs, goats, cows, horses, and sheep.

They could roam around at night, quietly, finding their meals in the dark.

Hunting.

When day light would break, they would return to the water and sleep during the day. And wait.

Tonight, as the Ehren family slept inside, these things climbed out of the water, looking for food. They had a keen sense of smell, picking up on every scent the wind brought them. Tonight, on this farm, they smelled meat.

They usually traveled in pairs, one being on the lookout for any potential threats, the other to hunt.

Under the cover of night, they made their way to the barn, the moonlight bouncing off their skin, illuminating the dark green color. They entered the barn from the partially opened double doors on the side where the wooden fence was. The small animals made a *pitter-patter* sound as they scurried away.

The one who came to hunt used the claw from its index finger to slit the throat of two sleeping goats. The goats fell over quickly, the blood swirling in the dirt turning it into dark brown mud. Other animals bounced into each other, trying to get out of the way. They each grabbed one, flung it over their shoulders, and headed back to the pond.

A group of four headed south, and another group of six headed west, looking for more bodies of water. They were here.

CHAPTER 6

Garland Creek ran through the southern part of town, from West to East, snaking through the woods, eventually flowing into Raymond River. Several man-made walking trails had been carefully trenched through the woods, all leading to the creek, most making their way alongside it as a perfect companion for hiking.

Over the years, teenagers had used the dense woods for a night out with friends for underage smoking or drinking. Occasionally, teenagers would use it as a get away from their parents and do some serious necking (*Oh, babe. Of course, I will still love you and respect you tomorrow.*)

A flashlight danced and bounced around as Derek Hudson and Brittany Meltzer walked towards the creek, Brittany falling in love with Derek, or so she had thought recently since they had started dating. She dated him mainly to piss off her father, who didn't want her to date anyone, but she liked Derek, and he was popular. In high school, that's half the battle to gaining your own notoriety and recognition.

Derek had passed her a note in Mrs. Stierwalt's Geometry class, asking her out. She was immediately offput by the horrible grammar and spelling, and she wanted to laugh. She could sense him watching her, though, so she kept it inside.

"Can you meet me somewear tonight?" He had written. She cringed at the misspelling.

She wrote back, *"Yes."*

That night, they made their way to the part of the creek where a slight waterfall splashed down, leaving a white foam at its base, and where they could face the trail coming towards them, so they couldn't be caught in the act. Derek didn't care if they were.

Derek, who had been carrying a blanket under his right arm, unfolded it, flipped it in the air, and then placed it on the ground.

"I think this is a good spot. What do you think?" he said, not planning on going anywhere else.

"Fine with me," she said, pulling out her phone to check the time. "Are you sure no one will be out here this time of night?"

"Brittany, we're fine. I have been coming here for a long time. It's always dead quiet this time of night," Derek said, trying to reassure her.

"For a long time, huh? Just how many girls have you brought out here?" she said, putting her phone in her back pocket.

"That's not what I mean. Travis and I used to come out here all the time and smoke. No one is ever here past dark."

He sat down on the blanket, looked up at Brittany, and patted the spot beside him, inviting for her to sit with him. He grabbed her flashlight and turned them both off.

"You're lucky you're cute," she said, sitting down beside him.

"I'm even more lucky to be with you," he said, smiling, then slowly closed in for a kiss.

She accepted, closing her eyes, and the two began kissing. Brittany reached up, grabbed a fistful of Derek's hair on the back of his head, and pulled him in closer to her.

He put his hand on her leg.

Their eyes were closed, and their lips were pressed together when the sound of a stick (*snapping?)* breaking made them both jerk away from each other and look around.

"What was that?" Brittany said, turning on her flashlight as she stood.

Derek, still sitting on the blanket, looked around. He smiled. "Babe, there are a lot of animals out here. I'm sure it was just a squirrel or something. Come here."

Brittany didn't look at him, flashing her light around like one of those guys who direct planes on the runways.

Someone jumped out of the woods and screamed.

"Shit!" Derek yelled, now on his feet.

It was Travis.

Travis said, "I knew you two would be out here!"

"You're a jerk," Brittany said, sitting back down on the blanket.

"Not cool, man," Derek said, then checked his phone. He gave Travis the *"what are you thinking interrupting what I have going on here?"* look.

"Oh, relax. You guys didn't even make it to second base yet. I was watching," Travis said, now turning on a flashlight of his own.

"You sicko! You were watching us?" Brittany said with a look of disgust on her face.

"Just for a minute," Travis said, his smile fading.

"Dude, get out of here," Derek said, playfully pushing Travis. Travis stumbled backward.

A sound came out of the woods to their left, sounding larger than a squirrel. This sounded more like a human. The three of them turned toward it in unison.

"Derek, take me home. I want to get out of here," Brittany said. He could hear the fear in her voice as it quivered.

They didn't notice the eyes watching them carefully.

Travis, closest to the entry to the woods, had his back to it. Something grabbed him by the shoulder, pulling him into the woods, violently. He didn't have a chance to scream.

"Travis!" Derek said, then to Brittany, "Come on!"

Leaving the blanket behind, their flashlights now swirling like strobe lights, they ran away from the creek, toward where they had come in.

A crashing sound echoed off the trees as Derek was pulled into the woods, his flashlight going end over end, landing on the bank of the creek. It shut off as it hit the ground.

Brittany, now alone, tried to scream but couldn't get anything to come out. Tears were now streaming down her face as she kept running away toward the parking lot. She was still far enough away that she could only see the surrounding trees.

Adrenaline working its magic, giving her a cardiovascular boost, allowed her to inch closer to the exit of the woods quickly. Yellow eyes appeared behind a row of bushes. It reached for her. She screamed this time as she fell to the ground. The flashlight fell to the ground with a thud, shining its light into the row of bushes. She was shaking. Something grabbed her by the hair and pulled with so much force it ripped her dark hair from her scalp.

In the flashlight's beam, you could see a dark green hand pulling her deeper into the woods.

CHAPTER 7

It was a pleasant night of sleep. Garrett slept the whole night through. It was the type of sleep where he couldn't remember falling asleep and couldn't remember if he had had a dream or not. It was the kind of sleep nature intended. Rejuvenating would be the ideal word for it. The kind of sleep where you wake up in the exact same position you fell asleep in.

As the sun was just starting to show the dew glistening on the summer grass, Garrett opened his eyes. He could have slept at least an hour longer, he thought, had it not been for the two birds outside his window chirping the morning away, singing their harmonious song. Waking up early on the weekend feels so different and so much better than waking up early on a weekday for work. He couldn't help but smile as he rolled over toward his nightstand to grab his phone. He had missed a text from Dave around midnight that stated, "*Told ya.*" Apparently, the baseball rivalry banter couldn't wait until Monday. Garrett, not amused, put his phone down and rubbed his eyes. He thought about Dave and how he was probably just starting a full night of online poker at midnight.

What a life.

Garrett sat down at the kitchen table, opting for a banana this morning. He was thinking only about the yardwork and wanted to get a jump start on it before it got too hot. The banana had started to turn brown, just the way he liked them. Softer, with more flavor. As he ate, he opened up social media and went to Laura's Instagram. Around the same time that Dave had texted him putting down his Tigers, Laura posted three pictures of her and a girlfriend eating at a new restaurant downtown. Garrett felt a wave of relief run through him when he saw Laura was with another girl. She currently had no guy in her life, he thought, and hoped it stayed that way.

He finished his banana, throwing the peel in the trash as he chewed the last delicious bite. He walked back to his bedroom and threw on an old white shirt and gray gym shorts he had worn several times to do yard work. The clothes had stains in them he never could get out, and his finger poked through a hole in the shirt as he unfolded it.

The garage door hummed and slowly began to rise when he hit the opener on the wall as he stepped inside. The opening door let the morning sun creep into the back of the garage, and it illuminated everything on the back wall, throwing shadows behind him. Garrett reached for his gardening gloves, moving his golf clubs out of the way to get to them. He had been meaning to get back into golf, having played on the high school team all four years. Since he graduated high school, he had only played a handful of times. He moved his golf bag out of the way, thinking maybe this was the year he would get back into it.

Why not?

He stepped outside, realizing today would be another hot day. He looked over to his right, towards the Klein residence, to see if they were sitting outside. It surprised him when he saw the front porch empty. Glancing at his watch, he supposed they were probably inside, eating breakfast and watching the morning news. It was only 7:30 am, and it was Saturday, the best day to sleep in.

To the left of Garrett Bradley's house, the same side that had the tulip tree, lived the McPherson's. They were an extremely nice couple, just a few years older than Garrett. Chad McPherson, the husband and father, was a firefighter for the Fullerton County Fire Department. His wife, Alyssa McPherson, was a very attractive, petite blonde who was an elementary school teacher for Lake Grove Elementary school, where their two children attended. Gideon, their son, was an eight-year-old boy with blonde, almost white hair who played outside as often as he could and loved football. If he and his dad weren't outside throwing a football or baseball, Gideon could be found somewhere in the neighborhood riding his bike. Their daughter, the youngest member of the McPhersons, was five-year-old Abby, who had long brown hair and was the spitting image of her father. She was always shy and quiet, and she loved her two cats, Snowy and Mittens. Almost every time Abby was seen, she was holding one of them. Most nights, they slept in her bed with her, and she'd fall asleep once they'd stop purring in her ear.

Garrett started toward the side of the house closest to the McPherson residence, assessing how long pulling the weeds would take him. He walked around the corner and stared at the area he wanted to tackle today. Garrett walked back to his garage to grab a shovel. The blade made a metallic *ding* as he pulled it off the hook on the wall. He glanced back over on the other side of his house and noticed the front porch was still empty at the Klein's.

Doing quick math in his head, Garrett compared his mental notes with a visual check to see how many bags of rock he guessed it would take to cover this side up against his house. He enjoyed doing the physical work but didn't really care for landscaping. He stood there, taking his mental notes, then got down on his knees to pull some weeds. A bead of sweat had already formed on his forehead and upper lip. A saying his dad always said popped into his mind.

"It wouldn't be so hot, but it's the humidity that gets ya."

Realizing he would need a wheelbarrow to make things easier for all the weeds and rock he would be buying, Garrett stood up, wiped his forehead, and headed towards his backyard, towards the small shed he had near the back of his fence. The shed was small, but he kept some equipment in there, including his wheelbarrow and push mower. Every time he opened the doors to his shed, there was a distinct smell of gasoline, a smell of fresh-cut grass, and the smell of old plastic.

He opened the creaking wooden door to a loud crash as his weed trimmer fell to the floor, echoing loud in the small shed.

"Good Lord," he said out loud, as he jumped back as if the trimmer was listening and had purposely played a prank on him. "Better that than a snake," he said to himself and laughed.

He was pulling off his right gardening glove with his left hand as he was shutting the shed door with his right leg. He squinted at the sun, and it reminded him to grab his sunglasses. Garrett pushed his privacy fence door open, stepped out, and turned to close it. As he turned towards his garage to get his sunglasses, he noticed Chad was outside doing something in his garage. The two men waved to each other.

"Mornin," they both said simultaneously.

Garrett grabbed his sunglasses off his workbench and walked back to grab the wheelbarrow sitting by the side of his privacy fence. The temperature was rising, and Garrett began to sweat more. He put both hands on the handles of the wheelbarrow and felt the rough edges. Something at the back edge of his property, where his fence line and the McPherson's property met, caught his eye. At first glance, it looked like someone had left a white sweatshirt on the ground. He figured it belonged to Gideon or Abby, so he would grab it and hand-deliver it to Chad before he got back to his yard work. Getting closer, he noticed there were also streaks of pink and red on the white sweatshirt that sat in the brutal morning sun. Garrett's face hardened, and he stopped. The sweatshirt he thought he saw had formed into a clearer image, and he narrowed his eyes. It wasn't a sweatshirt; it was a cat. There, in the wet grass, lay one of Abby's best friends, Snowy, mutilated and what looked to be half-eaten. More than half of the body was gone. Most of the skull was showing, a white-gray reflecting in the sun. Snowy's tongue was swollen and protruding. There had been a perfect tear down the middle of the abdomen that exposed the intestines. The liver was decimated to about a quarter of its original size. Garrett pressed his lips together, then sighed as he realized he would have to deliver the news to Chad, who would have to deliver it to his little girl.

Glad it's not me.

Trying to find the words and tact, Garrett walked with his head hung low to Chad, who was fixing the chain on Gideon's bike. A set of tools lie neatly on the garage floor next to him.

"What's happenin?" Chad said as he looked up at Garrett.

"Hey, uhh. Morning. Uhh. I…" Garrett said, sounding like a junior high thirteen-year-old trying to ask a girl out.

"What's up? You okay?" Chad said as he stopped working on his son's bike. He set a tool down, and it clanged on the garage floor.

"I'm sorry. I think I saw your cat at the back of our property. I think something killed her," Garrett said and felt horrible. He had guilt, or something like it, in his stomach, like he had been the one who was responsible for it.

"You're kidding me," Chad said as he stood up. His face turned to stone as he and Garrett both walked back of the yard in single file, Chad leading. He wiped the sweat from his forehead.

As they came upon Snowy, what was left of her, Chad turned around and looked at the back of his house, dreading the horror and sadness this would cause today. Chad had never been close to the cat, but he knew this would destroy everyone else. He knelt down by her.

"Coyotes! I saw a few last week in the field behind our house. Abby's gonna have a fit. Alyssa will, too," Chad said as he stared at the back of his house. He stood and grimaced.

"I'm sorry. Anything I can do?" Garrett said uncomfortably.

"No, I appreciate it. I'll bury her really quick, so the girls don't see this mess. Thanks for letting me know. This ain't gonna be fun telling them this."

Garrett still had a sick feeling spinning through him as he walked back to his wheelbarrow and the yard work that was still waiting for him. He had this strange feeling inside of him, and he wasn't sure why. Something seemed off. He bent over to pull weeds but couldn't. He couldn't get the image of that bloody mess of a cat out of his mind. For some reason, he didn't think a coyote had killed that cat. He was right.

Chapter 8

After breakfast, Jake Ehren went upstairs and began to type, the clicks seeming to get faster every day. Jake recently had found an author that he really enjoyed reading, which, in turn, made him want to be a writer himself. He had been setting aside at least an hour a day to perfect his craft.

He had recently started an online blog, "Life On The Farm," about the day-to-day dullness of living on a farm in a small town, where the most exciting thing that happened was a runaway goat. He wrote under the pen name "FarmLivin2005."

His blog didn't attract many readers, but he enjoyed being able to put his thoughts down for others to enjoy, dreaming one day of being a famous author. Had he known what was lurking in the pond he fished in almost every morning, he would have been able to spice up the blog a bit.

Today he rambled, struggling to find the words to describe the last twenty-four hours on the farm. He fed the animals, argued with his brother, helped his father clean out the back room of the old barn, and helped his mom with a few chores inside.

"*This is so stupid. No one is going to want to read this crap*," he said to himself.

He stood up, put his hands on the back of his head, and stretched. He paced around his room, trying to think of ways to enhance his writing. He looked at his bookshelf, assuring himself he would never make it as a writer. Frustration and anger mixed and boiled.

He sat down on his bed, now down in the dumps about his passion for writing. His mind wandered back to the time he convinced his parents to get him a guitar for Christmas, which they did, and he quit playing in less than a year. He taught himself a few chords, his fingers always struggling with placement. When he was finally able to get the placement down, he struggled with strumming with his other hand.

He looked over at his guitar that sat in the corner like an old friend who missed him dearly. Seeing it made guilt, anger, and sadness swirl from his stomach to his head. He looked away, the guilt too much. He balled his hands into fists and slammed them down into his bed.

Outside, a bubble rose to the surface of the pond and popped.

CHAPTER 9

Fourteen miles away, in the small town of Adelco, the invasion had begun on a small cabin on a lake, three miles away from any type of civilization. Jeff and Sarah Nielsen had built this cabin about six years ago, never wanting kids, opting for a peaceful life where they decided they would try to live "off-grid" as much as possible. Jeff was an electrician by trade but hadn't had a job in two years. They had lived off some money he got in a lawsuit settlement when, driving down the interstate, he was struck by another vehicle of a couple who had gotten into an argument, the wife jerking the steering wheel out of the husband's hands, crashing into Jeff and putting him in a coma. He had walked slightly hunched over and had a visible limp ever since that accident. These days, Sarah worked part-time at the hardware store off of State Road 22, needing something to do and people to talk to a few days a week. Sarah loved Jeff, but their relationship had become strained over the last two years since his accident.

Sarah had noticed the change when Jeff had become addicted to painkillers not long after the accident that gave him his limp. His back and legs had ached constantly, sending sharp, fiery pain up the back of his legs into his lower back. When Sarah noticed that Jeff had been sleeping more and more, she confronted him about his pill addiction. It was the only time in their relationship he had become physical, pushing her up against the wall in their bedroom without remorse. He had a miserable, sick feeling for days when he had done that to her.

They've worked on things recently, but there was still something in her mind that never went away. Did she want to leave? At times, yes. Did she hate him? At times, yes. But she loved him, and the thought of leaving her comfort made her chest hurt. She didn't want to leave her lake, her cabin, or her life with Jeff, but somewhere in her psyche, she knew she would never feel the same about him.

As she read a book in bed, she was unaware she was being watched. She had been watched for over twenty-four hours now.

These *things* would silently and stealthily watch their victims for a few days to see which ones would be easy targets. They would first prey on the easy ones that would not put up a fight; small children, the elderly, and the incapacitated.

These creatures were clever. They had the ability to take on the form of whatever they touched. They could sneak up on you anywhere, touch anything around you, and become that object. They could get close to you without you knowing it. It was an effective way to have the element of surprise on anyone or anything. They had the upper hand.

When they arrived on Earth, specifically the Ehren farm, their mission was simple; take it over. They were very large. They stood about seven feet tall. They were a dark, almost black and green color, and their eyes glowed yellow. They had a distinct smell; a musty smell of mildew. They had enormous feet and hands, the size of an NBA basketball player's, or maybe even larger than that. Their intent wasn't to kill *(yet)*, their intent was to inhabit and gain information to see if Earth was an inhabitable place.

This hadn't been the only planet. There are others out there.

They had a cruel, quick way of putting humans into what is essentially a coma. Once they placed their large, swampy-smelling hands on their victim's head, all brain activity altered. It didn't stop functioning, but it didn't function properly. Humans would go to sleep like they had been anesthetized, having no inkling of what was happening around them. It was cruel, but it happened instantaneously, usually before the victim realized what was happening to them. Just the slightest pain, then deep sleep.

They have the upper hand.

Then they formed into that human, a perfect likeness. No one would be the wiser. They incorporated their thoughts, their feelings, their desires, and their history. So, it was true, once Sarah's brain activity changed from normal to catatonic, which this *Being* had every intention of doing, it could walk out into the living room to Jeff, feel everything she ever felt for Jeff, know everything she had ever known about Jeff, tell Jeff she wanted a goodnight hug and kiss, and easily drop his body on the floor. No thought about it, no question. No feelings. Goodnight.

Sayonara.

Sarah was deep into the novel she was reading, the way you get into a good book that seems to hit close to home. She was currently enjoying a series by an author from New England who specialized in pulling on the heartstrings of women in their 50s, the love stories that always seemed to have happy endings. Usually, the story involved a woman who had gone through a terrible divorce, only to find that her knight in shining armor was her single, quiet neighbor who you always rooted for in the beginning, the reader screaming at her for not being able to see it for herself.

She sat upright in her bed, reading about fall in New Hampshire, and she envisioned the leaves changing from green to all the fall-like colors, wishing herself swept away by an unsuspecting next-door neighbor dreamboat. She glanced up just in time to see a dark object coming at her head. Before she could even understand what she was looking at, before she could even let out a scream or cry for help to Jeff, the dark green moldy smelling hand was already on her. She never had a chance. The B*eing* quickly picked her up and placed her on the floor. These things needed their victims to stay alive to have the ability to take their shape and incorporate their thoughts. That's why they didn't plan on killing (*yet*). Once their humans were no longer useful to them, then they could kill them. But until then, they used their bodies to do and get what they needed, and then it was on to the next set of victims.

Jeff sat in the living room half asleep, watching the local news with a small glass of bourbon he had been sipping on all evening. Sarah had noticed within the last few weeks that his drinking had gotten out of control. *Just a few sips here and there to ease his pain, to get away from reality for a while*, is usually what Jeff told himself. Besides, he deserved it. He had worked hard his whole life. He came from a broken family with an abusive father. He was allowed to enjoy the company of a stiff drink here and there. He couldn't care less what Sarah thought, and he had been more than happy to tell her that a few times over the last week or two.

As he nodded off to sleep and his leg fell off the small stool he used to prop his legs up, Sarah walked into the living room.

"I know what you're thinking," Jeff said as he pushed his glasses up over his eyes. "It was just one drink. My back is really bothering me tonight."

Sarah just stared at Jeff, not saying a word. Jeff stared back and, for the first time, he felt like he hated her. Even for a brief second, he wondered what it would be like if she just went away and he had the place to himself without having to look at her. He almost felt nothing for her anymore. Sarah walked up to him, still staring, as he propped himself up in his chair, grimacing at the pain in his lower back.

"It's fine, sweetie. Enjoy your drink," Sarah said, smiling, but not her usual smile.

Jeff half-smiled back as Sarah placed her hand on the top of his head. He slowly fell to the floor as bourbon spilled all over the wall and carpet.

CHAPTER 10

Garrett had finished the yardwork he wanted to complete, although even he would admit it wasn't satisfactory. His heart wasn't in it after what he witnessed with his neighbor's cat. After putting away all the gardening tools in the shed, he stood in his garage and noticed the sky was slowly turning a light gray color, and the air had gone from warm and humid to a slight, cool breeze. He walked out to his mailbox, not remembering if he had checked his mail the previous day. The smell in the air was foul, like someone had placed fresh fertilizer out on their lawn. The smell made him think of the mauled cat.

Snowy. You were a good girl.

There was no mail, and he scratched his lower back as he shut the metal door of the mailbox. Stretching and hearing his back crack, he looked over and noticed Mr. Klein sitting on his porch. He would have bet all the money in his wallet he wasn't out there just a few seconds ago, but he couldn't be sure. He raised his hand to wave, giving him the neighborly wave and nod. Mr. Klein waved back with a look of confusion and uncertainty. There was no expression on his face as he stared at Garrett. Garrett did a double-take and squinted, wondering if the Klein's had just had an argument. He looked down at his driveway, trying to picture an elderly couple fighting. He half grinned, thinking how amusing it would be to see them yelling at each other. Then, in his mind, he imagined what the Kleins were like when they were younger. Surely, they went through the same marital strains that everyone goes through. He imagined Mr. Klein asking Mrs. Klein out on a date, having a hard time picturing it in his brain. He pictured Mr. Klein with darker hair and younger eyes, hoping to get to third base, secretly wanting to steal home, and that made him laugh out loud.

The McPherson front door shut, and that snapped Garrett out of his daydream. Alyssa McPherson walked out of their house and was heading toward her white minivan. She noticed Garrett standing in his driveway and he could tell she had been crying. Garrett looked at her with an *"I know you've been crying and I am so sorry"* look, and she nodded her head as if they understood what each other was saying with their non-verbal glances. Alyssa grabbed something out of the minivan and headed toward the house. Seeing her like that put the pit back in Garrett's stomach. He had to look away and turn back around toward the Klein house. Mr. Klein was no longer sitting on his front porch.

Garrett's mind shifted from the Klein's to Laura, and a wave of emotion shot through him like a seventh-grader who had just been handed a love note. He had wanted to message her again, but fought it with everything he had. He swatted at a fly that had buzzed by his ear and again looked up at the Klein's front porch. It threw Garrett off to see Mr. Klein back on his porch, staring at Garrett, a smile on his face. Garrett turned back around and headed for the garage.

What Garrett didn't realize was these things were closing in.

Can't you feel them here? Can't you feel them circling in?

Last night the Klein's didn't stand a chance. As they slept, they were taken over, an easy target for their midnight visitor. The couple, who almost always fell asleep holding hands, didn't awaken to see the piercing yellow eyes staring at them. The *Being* had no sympathy for the couple. They were easy. It placed its oversized hand on Mr. Klein's head and finished her off shortly after. There was no pain. It was peaceful.

CHAPTER 11

A local news channel was on in a dimly lit living room. The old man slept as the light from the screen reflected off his glasses.

"Authorities are asking for help to find three missing teens. According to police, seventeen-year-olds Derek Hudson, Brittany Meltzer, and Travis Alexander were last seen July 29th."

Their photographs were displayed on the screen.

"Hudson's vehicle was found parked at the north side of Garland Creek. The police department says it has been working with the families since they were reported missing. Anyone with information on their whereabouts is asked to contact the phone numbers or email on the bottom of the screen."

CHAPTER 12

One crawled its way out of the Ehren pond. It flexed, opening its hands and moving its fingers. Pond water dripped off of them. Its foot found the mud on the bank and sunk down with a *squoosh* sound.

It looked around outside, looking first toward the field, then toward the Ehren home. All the lights were out. Its feet walked across the gravel, making a popping sound. In one motion, it leaped up the side of the Ehren home. It found a bedroom window and peered in. Jake's room. It put its hand up to the window, transformed, and was standing next to Jake's bed within seconds. A hand was placed on Jake's head. The light from his computer threw a shadow on the wall. His blog was up, and the cursor flashed, patiently waiting for more strokes of the keyboard.

CHAPTER 13

The evening brought a cold rain to central Michigan. The foul smell still hung in the air, like a rug that had been left outside to mold. Garrett opened his phone, eager to check Laura's social media. He still had the pit in his stomach, making him feel extremely nauseous, and he felt more alone than usual tonight. Garrett had been following Laura's social media account for almost as long as he knew her, even though he didn't like mixing business and pleasure.

Tonight, as the rain beat against the windowpane, he had an incredible longing for her he couldn't describe. He was good at keeping business out of personal life, but tonight he couldn't seem to separate the two, or maybe he was over separating the two. For the first time since following her, he brewed up enough courage to message her. Deep down, he knew he shouldn't, but he wanted her more than he cared about the consequences. Life is funny that way. Just go for it and everything else be damned. Whatever the risks were, it didn't matter.

We'll deal with that later.

Garrett saw she had posted she was out with that same girlfriend of hers to see a movie that Garrett had no interest in seeing, something about a group of girls who go on a road trip across the country, one finding true love, and the other girls then help her plan a wedding. *Pluck my eyes out with a butter knife*, Garrett thought to himself.

I'm not waiting any longer.

He started typing on his phone.

How was the movie? Looked like an instant classic, he wrote.

"Stupid," he said out loud.

Garrett shook his head in an embarrassing type of disbelief.

Slick one, Romeo.

He let his head drop to his pillow, staring at the ceiling, instantly regretting the message. He could still hear the bitter rain tapping on the window like a soothing metronome. He stared at his phone for a few seconds, waiting for a response. Nothing. His throat immediately felt like it was full of sawdust. He kicked his feet and threw the blankets off of him, heading towards the kitchen to grab a bottle of water. He grabbed the cold bottle out of the fridge, downing half of it in a matter of seconds. Feeling better, he put the cap back on the bottle, tossed it in the air, caught it, and walked back to his bedroom.

Still no response. He rubbed his eyes and frowned, knowing he had crossed the proverbial line in which one does not mix business with pleasure.

I blew it.

He put his phone on his nightstand with a look of disgust in his eyes and sat up in bed, realizing his mistake. His phone lit up and went off with a ding. She had responded.

I can't tell if you are being serious or sarcastic, she wrote back.

He smiled, and his heart began to thud in his chest. He thought to himself, "*should I respond right away? I don't want to seem desperate*", but he no longer cared and wasn't interested in mind games.

Oh, I am so serious, he wrote with a smiley face emoji.

Well, then maybe you should have come, she replied.

Maybe you should have invited me, Garrett wrote back. "*What am I doing?*" he said to himself. But there was something in him that couldn't stop. Something about this conversation made him feel needed and wanted for the first time in….he couldn't remember how long. He could no longer help himself.

Laura replied, *Maybe I should have*, with a wink emoji. Garrett knew the time was now. He had to strike while the iron was hot. *Get while the gettin's good.* Forget about the workplace romance, what people will say, what they will think, how they will be viewed, and just go for it. *How about we start with dinner tomorrow night?* Garrett wrote. His heart was beating so hard he could feel it in his ears.

214 McCullen Lane, 6:30? Laura wrote.

Sounds like a date. Want to go to the new Italian place downtown? he messaged back. Laura replied, *It's a date. See you at my place at 6:30,* with a happy face emoji.

Garrett sat up in bed and did a fist pump like he had just thrown the winning touchdown pass. *See you then!* He wrote back. He started pacing around his bedroom.

Garrett was riding high and was unsure if he could even fall asleep right away, but he put his head on his pillow and fell asleep immediately.

Next door, the McPherson children's bodies lie still on the floor while their parents lay in their bedroom down the hall. Garrett was running out of time.

CHAPTER 14

The phone rang, and Jerry Bradley turned the volume down on the news channel he had been watching since he had his morning toast and coffee about an hour ago. Angela sat at the kitchen table in a robe that had seen better days, doing a crossword, looking deep in thought. On the second ring, Jerry stood up to grab the phone. He had been hoping Angela would walk over and grab it, but she had no intention of doing so. He watched for her to make the first move, but she didn't. He walked toward the ringing phone.

She had easily guessed "Alda" for 1 down (*Actor Alan*), but was chewing on the end of her pen, unsure of 4 down (*Cleopatra's Snake*).

"Hello?" Jerry said into the phone, looking out the window at the trees on a very bright Sunday morning.

"Hey, pops," Garrett almost yelled into the phone, still riding high from his messaging romance last night with Laura.

"Hey, boy," Jerry said back to him, still looking out the kitchen window. Angela looked up from her crossword and set her pen down on the table. It wasn't unusual for Garrett to call, but her maternal instinct perked up and she couldn't help but think something was wrong with her only child, especially since he was calling at 9 am.

"I just wanted to give you guys a little good news. I have a date tonight, so tell mom she can get off my back for a while."

"A date?" Jerry said as he shot a glance at Angela. Angela stood up with a smile she wasn't trying to hide, walked over to Jerry, and put her ear up to the phone. Jerry turned the phone outward so they both could hear.

"Yes, but dad, don't get too excited. It's a girl I work with, and I have known her for a while, but we are just going to get some dinner. I'm not getting married, and I'm not in love, so relax."

Half grinning, Jerry replied, "Tell that to your mother."

Angela said excitedly into the phone, "Garrett, I am so happy. It's about time!"

Laughing, Garrett said, "I know, mom. I am looking forward to it but calm down. It's really nothing. I will call you guys this evening and let you know how it went. But like I said, relax!"

"We're calm, boy," Jerry said into the phone. "I will make sure to keep your mom from going nuts, if that's even possible. We may be too late," he said, winking at Angela.

"Thanks, pops. I will chat with you both tonight. I love you both."

"We love you," Angela almost yelled into the phone. "Don't forget to call us back with details."

"Ok, love you both," Garrett said. They could somehow hear him smiling into the phone.

"Love you," Jerry said. There was a beep as the conversation ended. Jerry and Angela Bradley stood there smiling at each other, excited about the day's news from their only child.

"I knew it would happen sooner or later," Jerry said to his wife. She smiled excitedly.

Jerry walked over to the sink and rinsed his blue coffee mug from the morning's coffee. Angela sat down and looked down at her crossword, triumphantly smiling, having a hard time focusing.

Garrett looked outside and noticed the clear sky, too overwrought to think about anything than his date with Laura. Turning on the light in the bathroom, he checked his face in the mirror. He pursed his lips, raised an eyebrow, and lowered it, then did the same to the other. He thought about what he would say to Laura. He thought about what he should wear. His palms began to sweat with anxiety as he thought about what version of himself he would put out there tonight. Funny thing, isn't it? When people first meet and they start dating, they always put their best foot forward. You almost always get the best version of someone at first. It isn't until later you realize they are slobs. That they do little things like leaving their towels on the bathroom floor after a shower. Those small, meaningless little things that slowly drive you insane over time.

But that was for another day. For now, Garrett was going to be the hero. He was going to come in and sweep this girl off her feet, and maybe they would live happily ever after. He'd be the hero in a romance novel, where the cover showed a shirtless guy with long hair riding a white horse. As he stood there looking in the bathroom mirror, more than anything at that particular moment, he felt thankful. He had a good career, made more than enough money to do essentially whatever he wanted, and he had a date with a beautiful girl.

Good things are happening. Finally.

Angela had given up on her crossword, wondering how anyone could ever guess all the correct answers. They were always too difficult for her, but she never stopped buying them at the supermarket, where they were conveniently placed at eye level, right before you check out. You had to have knowledge of a vast number of categories to be able to complete these. She seemed to do well in the entertainment category, but struggled with the rest. She sat at the kitchen table, still beaming with excitement at the thought of Garrett finally going out on a date. She couldn't even recall when his last date had been. Her mind wandered to the time he was five, and he had cried one night because he wanted to "live with mommy and daddy forever." That almost made her tear up, but her happiness and the way the sun was shining through the skylight wouldn't allow her to feel that type of sadness.

Jerry had gone up to shower and brush his teeth to "*start the day*" as he called it. Angela stared at the television, realizing they had had the same Sunday routine for twenty years or so. All the emotions came pouring in and she hadn't remembered a morning where she had felt this happy in a long time.

Jerry came downstairs and smiled at his wife, wearing the same clothes he had on yesterday.

"Didn't you wear that shirt yesterday?" she said, with a hint of absurdity in her voice. Jerry smiled and nodded, and Angela noticed a hint of peculiarity. "And you're going to wear it again today?" she asked incredulously.

"I believe I will," Jerry said, still smiling. Angela frowned and got up to put her coffee mug in the sink. As she stood there waiting for the water to get hot, she could feel Jerry standing right behind her. She fell to the floor.

Outside, the birds chirped, and the sound of a lawnmower echoed in the air. The national news was still on the television with a bald man's face getting red as he discussed gas prices and the economy. Upstairs, on a perfectly made bed, the thing dropped Angela next to her husband, then walked back downstairs.

CHAPTER 15

Garrett showered and shaved, threw on some clothes, and paced around his house thinking about this evening's date. He had almost made himself feel nauseous with nervousness.

"Flowers," he said as he walked down the hall.

Great idea.

No date could be complete without flowers. He grabbed his phone off the nightstand and looked up floral shops in the area. As he scrolled, he remembered that a math teacher in high school had a husband who owned a flower shop.

What was the name?

Becky's Flowers on the south end of town.

Yep, that's the one.

Finding it on his phone, he checked them out to find reviews and check pricing. Both were reasonable. He stepped into the kitchen to grab a bottle of water out of the fridge and made up his mind that a dozen roses sounded perfect for this evening. He was beaming as he hit the side button of his phone and dropped it in his pocket.

Outside, you could not have asked for a bluer sky. In the distance, you could hear the banging of a hammer as someone in the front of the subdivision was getting a new roof. Across the street, Brad Bayner was standing in his garage.

Brad was a single man that Garrett didn't know very well. He was a quiet neighbor who kept to himself, one that never took the time for small talk, never getting too personal or asking any questions. On the weekends, you would always see him standing out in his garage, working on something, beer in hand. Garrett wasn't even sure what Brad did for a living. He knew he was a man's man, though. Tough and rugged. Garrett always assumed he was a carpenter or some type of handyman. The sound of a circular saw or some type of power tool was constantly blasting in his garage, thundering out to the neighborhood. Brad was always wearing some sort of flannel shirt and carpenter pants. The kind of man who, if you looked closely, was probably missing a finger or something. Naturally, Brad had scars all up and down his hands and arms from years of some sort of construction project.

Garrett walked outside, eager to get to the floral shop. Eyes squinting from the sun, he looked up and noticed Brad outside in his garage.

Of course he is.

Garrett raised his hand in a half-hearted wave, and Brad stared at him as if he had never seen him before. Garrett's face formed a slight frown, and his forehead wrinkled, unsure of Brad's hesitation.

What's your problem? Did I do something to you?

It was the same thought you have when you can't remember if you were mad at someone because of something that happened in real life or in a dream.

After a few seconds, Brad slowly raised his hand and waved in a stolid, animatronic motion. The glare from the sun made it hard to tell, but he was sure there was zero emotion on Brad's face, almost as if Garrett was looking at a neighbor who was nothing more than a skeleton with deep black eye sockets that led to even more nothingness. Garrett stared and, for a second, thought about walking over to ask Brad if he was ok; the confused, frowning look was still plastered all over Garrett's face.

The next street over, an older, attractive redhead woman in a tank top and black yoga pants was walking a Golden Retriever, her ponytail flopping back and forth with each step. As she came up to a fenced-in backyard, a Rottweiler charged at her. The two dogs- the Rottweiler and her own- started barking at each other, neither one backing down, both acting as if they owned the neighborhood. Saliva hanging from their mouths flew everywhere in foamy strings.

The sound of the barking booming off the houses snapped Garrett back to reality. He looked around with the same thoughts as you do when you wake up somewhere new. *Where am I? Who am I? How did I get here?*

He glanced up again, looking at the beautiful blue sky, noticing he couldn't even see a cloud. He unlocked his car and thought about the roses.

CHAPTER 16

Garrett took the two-lane highway that desperately needed a repave, to the south end of Burnley. His radio was tuned in to talk radio this morning. On the car speakers, the governor discussed term limits and the future of education for children in Michigan. Garrett liked politics. He had briefly contemplated running for governor one day, imagining a world with a beautiful trophy wife at his side, two beautiful kids, and how he would woo the people of Michigan into thinking he would change their lives like no one else had done before. His naïve optimism of hope was short-lived and eventually turned into a pessimistic view of the whole political game. He thought about the homeless problem downtown. He thought about world hunger and how the poor stayed poor, but the rich got richer. Did anyone really get into politics to change things? Or did they enter the races to make a name for themselves? Lying to people, getting them to believe they were the ones that would save them, solve all the world's problems, and everyone would live in a world where everyone got along, had a little bigger piece of the pie, and had fewer worries. Where everyone sat around a campfire on some beach singing *kumbaya.* It was all bullshit. No one cared about you, and if you believed they did, then they had already won.

Garrett was solving the world's problems in his head while he listened to the governor play the Democrats vs. Republicans game, trying to rationalize which side was better suited to lead the state and country. Up ahead, he noticed the cars slowing down, coming to a stop. The right lane was slowing as everyone tried to make their way over to the left lane. Red turn signals flashed as a warning.

What's going on?

He sat more upright in his seat, straining his neck to peer over his hood, veering from left to right and back again, curious to see what was happening ahead. He thought he had seen something in the road, but couldn't make out what it was. The squiggly lines from the heat bounced off his hood, dancing in his line of vision. He inched closer, turning on his turn signal, trying to get into the left lane. He turned around to see if anyone would let him in. Up ahead, he hadn't noticed it earlier, but there was a police officer and a conservation officer directing traffic. Their vehicles were pulled off to the side with blue and red lights flashing in unison, as if they were Christmas lights on a timer with music.

He touched his brakes lightly to let an elderly couple in an old station wagon get in line before him. Garrett moved forward, looking out his right passenger window, and saw the mess in the road. Two deer lie in the road. One, a decent-sized buck, looked like it had been cut in half almost perfectly. Its head was looking towards Garrett as he slowly drove by. The buck's tongue, a white and slightly purplish red color, hung out of the right side of its mouth. A surprised, scared look had settled on its face, frozen in time to remain there forever. The other deer, a small doe, was almost unrecognizable. A brown, pink, and red glob of innards, meat, and hair lay in the road, making Garrett question if it was a deer or some other type of animal. Garrett raised his lips, scrunched his nose, and made a face as if he had just taken a big swig of spoiled milk.

Snowy the cat. These two deer.

As he passed, he looked up in the rearview mirror, noticing the conservation officer wearing black latex gloves. Garrett turned on his turn signal to enter back into the right lane, thankful to have a career that didn't include scraping decimated roadkill off of the pavement.

The rest of the ride was uneventful. Garrett had gone from talk radio to sports radio, then settled on a '70s and '80s country music station. Mel McDaniel was singing *"Big Ole' Brew"* as Garrett pulled into the parking lot of Becky's Flowers. The heat was still rising, the humidity was relentless. The sky was a perfect shade of blue.

The door to the shop opened with a jingle as two bells clanged together from the inside. It was 11:15 am.

"Good morning," the man behind the register said to Garrett. He was wearing a green apron, and had both of his hands sprawled out on the counter, leaning toward Garrett's direction. A towel was draped over his right shoulder.

"Good morning," Garrett replied, smiling.

"What can I help you with?" the man said as he stood tall, no longer leaning on the counter.

"Well, that's a good question. I find myself in uncharted waters today," Garrett said, walking up towards the counter.

The man showed a toothy smile, pulled a toothpick out of his mouth, and flicked it into the trash can behind him. He leaned forward, waiting for Garrett to go on.

"I have a date tonight, and I think I want to get a dozen roses. It seems…safe," Garrett said, unsure of the word he wanted to use.

The man grinned a wide grin, the corners of his mouth creasing, forming lines on his cheeks.

"Roses are always safe, young man. You know what they say? Dogs are man's best friend; roses are women's best friend." Garrett gave a courtesy laugh and nodded in agreement, but was sure he had never heard that phrase in his life. "I've got some beautiful red ones in the back. Give me about five minutes, and I'll have them out to you in a vase," the man said, stepping down from behind the counter, close to where Garrett was standing.

"Perfect, thank you," Garrett said, turning around, looking at the flowers and the different types of cards that were in perfect rows up and down the aisle.

Garrett walked down the aisle, looking at the different categories of cards written on a white laminated label. The cards, which all seemed to be red, pink, orange, and green, were in careful, deliberate groups. *"Thinking Of You," "Sympathy," "Congratulations," "Just Because," "Romance,"* and finally, *"I Love You."* Garrett read a few, turned around, and looked at the balloons, some tied with candy. He felt out of place at a shop like this. Showing a lot of emotion was never really his thing, and this place was wearing all sorts of emotions on its sleeve, naked and vulnerable. Garrett turned back to the cards, wanting to be done with this store and get back home. He laughed to himself, thinking how funny it would be to have a category called *"She Meant Nothing To Me."* He reached for one of the cards to read when he was interrupted by the man's voice.

"Ok, I think this will do the trick for you," the man said, walking by Garrett, but looking straight ahead at the counter. The man took the single step up next to the sign that read *"Employees Only."* He walked over to the register and wiped his forehead on his sleeve. "You're in luck. All of our flowers come in early Monday morning, so this was darn near all we had left," the man said as he pushed a few buttons on the register. "Usually, these are $59.99, but I'm in a good mood today. $49.99 will be your total, young man." Garrett did not know if he was being sarcastic, or if he was getting the Romeo and Juliet special, but he smiled and pulled out his wallet. The generosity made Garrett open up a bit.

"Are you Mrs. Long's husband? I mean, Mrs. Long that teaches at Burnley High School?" Garrett said as he pulled out his credit card.

"Yes, sir," the man said. "She's got two years left, or so she tells me. Then she says she's going to come work here with me. I mean, hell, she might as well. I named the place after her," the man said proudly.

Garrett smiled and said, "Tell her Garrett Bradley says hello. She was one of my favorite teachers." Garrett handed the man his credit card, and the man seemed grateful to hear something that kind about his wife of thirty-six years.

"I will tell her that. Appreciate you sayin' that," the man said as he rang Garrett up. The register beeped and made a humming noise as it spit out the receipt. The man ripped the paper off, wearing an expression like he had just heard a dirty joke. The man said to Garrett as he was handing the receipt to him, "Good luck tonight, kiddo." It was obvious he loved his job.

"Thanks," Garrett said with a smile he couldn't contain if he tried.

Garrett walked outside, unlocked his car, and carefully placed the vase on the floor on the passenger side of the car. As he shut the passenger door and started towards the driver's side, he noticed an elderly couple walking in, the older man holding the door open for his wife. The woman slowly walked in, slightly hunched over and holding a cane, and the old man looked at Garrett and winked. All was right in the world, and love was in the air.

Chapter 17

Garrett's car came to a slow stop in his driveway. He got out, shut the door, and looked around, amazed at the complete silence on the cul-de-sac. It was never this quiet here.

Something is off.

The Klein's were not sitting outside, the McPherson kids were not playing in their side yard, and the sound of some type of power tool was not coming from Brad Bayner's garage. Still looking around, confused, Garrett pulled out his phone to check the time. There was a message from Laura.

"I realized I never gave you my number," she wrote. *"524-892-3363. Will you text me when you are on your way? Thanks!"*

His heart started to thud a little harder, and his palms started to sweat again. The sweaty mix of anxiety and the heat hammering down like the beat of a drummer warranted another shower before tonight.

He responded, "*I'm 542-626-8702. I will text you when I head that way!*"

He felt like he was in high school again. He felt like it was prom night, and Garrett, the king, would be out with Laura, the queen. He shook his head and smirked, thinking about how his dad would always say, "*When your mom and I started going steady…*" When did people stop saying that, anyway?

Garrett caught a bit of Sunday afternoon baseball. The Braves were thumping the Nationals, and he scrolled through his phone, trying to waste time. He was checking email, swiping through social media, checking local and national news, anything he could to pass the time. A hot shower was a good way to move the hands of the clock forward.

He hopped in, half washing himself and half daydreaming about what was in store that evening. He figured if he could waste thirty minutes, he'd have enough time to get dressed, make himself look presentable, get some gas, and drive slowly over to Laura's. He stood, leaning against the shower wall, letting the water run through his hair and cascade down his back. The steam fogged the mirror above the sink, and he could no longer stare at himself in it.

He managed to waste almost fifty minutes, the time now almost 4:30 pm. He had two hours before he was supposed to get Laura, but if he got gas off the freeway, with traffic, he could waste about another forty-five minutes. He carefully put himself together, and the ladies would tell you he could put himself together well, walked outside, locked his front door, got in his car, and took off.

Here we go.

The freeway was down to one lane because of an accident, which he was morbidly thankful for because it let him waste another twenty minutes. Now, by the time he got gas and drove to Laura's, it would be close to 6:15 pm. He made it around the lane closure without incident, radio blasting, and took exit 24B East, turning towards the gas station. As he made the bumpy left turn into the parking lot, swerving around a few potholes, he noticed it had become dramatically cooler than it was when he had left home.

He pulled up to the pump, put the car in park, and got out as he hit the gas tank lid button next to the hood release. It clicked as it popped open. The wind, which went from non-existent earlier to now a very steady, cool breeze, gently lifted his perfectly combed hair on the right side. He checked it out in his driver-side window, then looked around to see if anyone noticed his subtle modesty.

A man in his mid-forties in a small SUV was pumping gas beside him, and the two men made eye contact. The man spoke up, "I don't know what's going on with this weather, man. It's been just about everything the last few days. It's crazy."

Garrett nodded his head in agreement and replied, "I know. Gotta love midwestern weather."

"If it were up to my wife, we would have moved to Florida ten years ago," the man said. Garrett paused and wet his lips.

"I guess it's not up to your wife then, huh?"

The man laughed and said, "Exactly. Exactly right, she…" Garrett and the man were interrupted by a woman who burst out of the gas station door, screaming incoherently, nearly falling over, followed by two men who were employees.

"Ma'am, you need to leave, or we will call the police."

"Call them. Let them all know," she yelled. Garrett and the man beside him glanced at each other and then back at the commotion.

"Why aren't you listening to me?" She exclaimed. "They are all coming. Some of them are already here. I've already seen them. They are big, and they are after us. They are after our children. Don't you get it? It's not safe! Don't trust anyone! All of you! We have to do something, or we will all be dead soon!"

"Ma'am, please," one employee said, escorting her to her car. He grabbed her arm.

"Get your hands off of me! You're dead, and you don't even know it! We all are! They are here. They are here, now!" She opened the door to her car and slammed it, still yelling something, but it was now muffled. The other employee stood behind her car, taking a picture of her license plate number, having every intention of calling the police.

55B5915. In God We Trust.

Garrett had walked about ten feet from his car, watching the commotion, unaware he had done so. The man beside him had done the same. As they turned to walk back to their cars, the man looked over at Garrett.

"And on that note, it's time for me to get out of here."

Garrett let out what tried to be a laugh, but he felt like he had cotton shoved down his throat. He coughed and swallowed and heard an audible click. "Same here. Stay safe," Garrett said to the man as they both entered their cars.

Garrett didn't feel right. The whole day had seemed off to him. The quietness of his neighborhood, the way the weather had ferociously changed minute by minute, and now the end of times crazy lady causing a scene at the gas station. Garrett started his car, made sure the flowers were still on the floor (*why wouldn't they be?*) and put his seatbelt on. He messaged Laura, *I'm heading your way*, with a smiley face.

CHAPTER 18

Garrett's anxiety was rising, ready to boil over, with every minute that passed. With every mile down, he was that much closer to starting his first date in God knew how long. But what was that lady at the gas station going on about? What did she mean, *"they were here?"* Garrett shook his head in perplexity and drove on. The world has some pretty crazy people living in it.

She's probably on drugs.

He slowed, checking the GPS on his phone, as he gradually drove down a one-way street, looking at the red brick condos. Laura's was the seventh one on the right. He turned into her driveway, exhaling, trying to slow his heart rate. Her front door was open, and he could see a light on in the window. He leaned over, exhaled once more, and picked up the flowers.

Here goes nothing.

He started up the stairs to her porch, painted gray, noticing the paint peeling with age. He wondered if he should offer to paint it for her, unsure of why he was thinking of that at this very moment. He looked up and was caught off guard seeing her stand there in a tan-colored dress, looking beautiful, smiling at him from behind the glass door. She looked at him and noticed the flowers in his hand. Her smile grew larger.

"Hey there," he said, his mouth as dry as the Sahara. "These are for you." His hands were trembling, and he could feel the sweat start to form on his palms.

Keep it cool. Keep it cool.

"Oh my goodness, these are beautiful," she said as she took them, followed by a sincere "Thank you."

He smiled, feeling relieved but still feeling anxious. At that moment, he wasn't sure he had ever seen her look that beautiful. He wasn't sure he had ever seen anyone look that beautiful.

"Come in and sit down for a minute. I need to close up before we can go," she said, turning around.

"Sure," he said back. He came inside, hands buried in his pockets, looking around. He was instantly struck by the aroma in the house. Did she just smell this good, or was she burning a candle? Her house smelled like fall, with an apple pumpkin mix that made him think of Thanksgiving. It was a sweet smell, not overwhelming the way some candles can be. He looked at the pictures on her wall as he sat on her brown sofa, which had a green blanket neatly folded on it. There were pictures of her looking younger, with who he assumed were her parents and a brother. He had always heard of looking at your girlfriend's mother because that's what you'll have in twenty-five years. He studied her mother's face and body in the pictures.

Not bad at all.

She walked into the kitchen, putting the flowers down on the counter next to her sink. She walked by again, disappearing into her bedroom, smiling at him as she passed. He couldn't tell if it was a nervous smile, but it was insanely seductive. Again, he noticed his throat was dry as he rubbed his hands together.

Laura walked out of the bedroom and said, "Ready to go?" as she raised her eyebrows. It was the first time he noticed just how green her eyes were. Inside, he was melting.

"Absolutely! Let's go," he said, standing up, instinctively checking to make sure he had his phone, wallet and keys.

"Can we just make one promise?" she said, picking up her purse and zipping it closed. "Can we not talk about work?"

"Really?" he said, looking at her, smiling. "I was hoping I could run some numbers by you and discuss the latest project I've been working on," he said, surprised at how well he kept a straight face.

She glanced back, at first unsure if he was serious. She rolled her eyes, then laughed and opened the door. "I don't even want to discuss work while I'm at work," she said, almost with an angry undertone.

"I hear you," he said, nodding his head. "No work tonight. That's an easy promise to keep."

After she turned the key to lock her door, she dropped her key chain into her purse, then they made their way down the steps to his car in the driveway. He followed her closely, still trying to play it cool. He had made up his mind earlier to open the car door for her, but he didn't want to seem too into her just yet. That would all come later. She could sense his ubiquitous apprehension.

He felt more at ease as they got into the car and took off for the restaurant. They made small talk, like where they went to school, what life was like growing up, and what their parents did for a living. He could tell his feelings for her were growing.

Already?

He could feel a deep-seated interest in her. It didn't hurt that she was stunningly attractive. It seems to be easier to have an interest in someone that you are attracted to. That's half the battle. He was smitten. Surreptitiously, he caught a few glances of her legs. They were perfect. His mind wandered on and on.

They pulled into the restaurant, then made their way inside. They both liked and appreciated the vintage style look it had. Red and white checkered tablecloths, servers walking around with classic style suits, the sounds of Dean Martin and Perry Como swooning over the old-looking speakers that hung in the corners of the room. He felt like he had stepped back in time when everything was black and white. He wondered momentarily if life was easier then.

The hostess, who couldn't have been over eighteen, led them to their tables, waiting for them to be seated before handing them their menus.

Bradley, party of two.

"Enjoy your dinner," she said, smiling, albeit uninterested. Garrett figured this was her summer job her parents forced her to take to help pay for college she didn't really even want to attend. The joys of being a teenager.

Garrett helped Laura into her seat. He sat, handed her a menu, then picked up the other one for himself. He turned it over, and the lights from above flashed off the laminated page.

"All of this sounds good. Well, at least what I can read. Some of these words are foreign to me," he said, not glancing up from the menu to see her expression.

Laura stared at him. She was completely lost looking at him. She was in a daze, awestruck at how she was getting a rush of feelings pulsing through her already. It was then, as her hands rested on the red and white checkered tablecloth, that she decided he was something worth pursuing. All of these emotions were swirling around inside her while he tried to figure out what focaccia bread was.

"I'm a simple girl," she said. "I want chicken parm."

His eyes rose from the menu to her. "Thank God. I have no idea what half of this stuff is. I'm getting spaghetti and meatballs," he said with relief. They both laughed.

The server came over soon after with two small glasses of water he placed in front of them.

"My name is Roberto," he said, as he almost did what would be considered a curtsy.

Garrett forcefully held back a bark of laughter and pretended to cough.

"Are you two ready to order?" Roberto said with a grin that seemed too wide for his face.

"I think we are," Garrett said, looking over at Laura for her approval. She nodded. Garrett held out his hand, palm up towards her, as a motion for her to go first.

"I will do the chicken parm, please," she said, so politely it killed Garrett inside.

"I'll do the spaghetti with meatballs," Garrett said as he handed the menu back to the server. "Oh, could I also do a bottle of the Pinot Noir?" Garrett asked.

The waiter again did the curtsy, or bow, whatever it was, and could tell that it was probably the first time "*Pinot Noir*" had ever been uttered from Garrett's lips. He took the other menu from Laura and turned around, headed toward the kitchen.

"So let me ask," Garrett said, now feeling more relaxed than he had all day. "Are you a baseball fan?"

Laura took a sip of water before answering. "I actually do like baseball. I don't really like watching the games on TV, but I love going to games," she said flirtatiously.

"I love doing both. But I agree, it's definitely more fun to go to a game. There's nothing better than a ballpark hot dog and a cold beer in hand," he said excitedly.

Laura thought it was cute how he perked up talking about baseball, like a little kid who told his mom he was picked to be student of the day at school. "Who's your team?" she asked, more to humor herself than anything.

"Tigers all the way!" he said with a childlike grin. "What about you?" he asked so seriously it almost made her giggle out loud.

"Sure… the Tigers," she said, laughing. He realized she liked baseball but didn't follow it at all. That made him snort a laugh.

"I'll take you to a game sometime, I mean…. if you want," he said, worried he was putting too much out there too soon.

Slow down, bro.

"I'd like that," she said, staring into his eyes.

The food came, they ate and drank a little wine, and everything was perfect. The night could not have gone any better. There was an undeniable chemistry between the two, and they couldn't seem to take their eyes off of each other. Garrett paid the bill to a thankful but still bowing Roberto, and he and Laura headed for the door. It was a successful first date, and Garrett was already thinking about what he would say when he called his parents at some point tomorrow.

Mom's gonna freak out.

The drive home was kind of quiet, two smitten people with bellies full of pasta and wine, the appropriate small talk still taking place. Her perfume hung in the air. The interstate seemed deserted. The headlights of an occasional passing car or semi-truck illuminated the inside of Garrett's car. Laura had already texted her best friend, telling her how the night had gone and that she hoped they would go out again.

They pulled into her driveway, both relieved to take off their seatbelts and give their full stomachs room to breathe. Garrett got out of the car, shut the door, and headed toward Laura's side, eager to open the door for her. She was already getting out of the car, surprised to see Garrett on her side, not used to having someone open a car door for her. She got out smiling and thanked him.

They walked up to her front door, and the moon, seeming larger than usual, reflected off his dark car. "I had a great time tonight," she said, looking into his eyes.

"So did I. Thanks for coming along. I couldn't tell you the last time I went out with someone," he said, almost embarrassed now. His heart was beating so hard that he was certain she could see it in his temples. He wasn't sure if he should lean in for a kiss or not, but knew it was now or never and leaned in toward her. She closed her eyes and fell into him, their lips pressing together. They said their goodnights, and Laura shut the door behind her, certain she had met Mr. Right.

Outside, Garrett stood on her front porch and no longer thought about it needing to be repainted. He looked up at the moon and smiled. Love was still in the air.

CHAPTER 19

Sandy Pickrell had lived in central Michigan almost her entire life. She had never married; she had never had a boyfriend. Come to think of it, she had never held hands with a boy, except for once in fifth grade when they had to learn to square dance. She had had a job once, when she worked twelve hours a week at the local Goodwill. The store manager had put her in charge of the book area, where she organized, alphabetized, and categorized better than any employee he had ever had. Then, on a cold and snowy Saturday morning, she decided that wasn't for her anymore and didn't show up for work. She didn't have the presence of mind to call her manager, who was about fifteen years younger than her, and tell him she wasn't coming back. No, Sandy just stopped coming in.

About a year later, just before Thanksgiving, she filed for disability. Her claim was, word for word, *"a persistent psychological and psychiatric disorder, causing emotional and mental distress, that adversely affects performance.*" What sort of mental illness this was, exactly, no one knew, but everyone did know that she was batty. She was the kind of person who dressed extremely eccentrically. Even on overcast, rainy days, she would have on 1969 Woodstock style sunglasses, the circular kind with pink or blue lenses, and would wear a top hat with a dress. Often, walking around her apartment complex or even stocking the books at Goodwill, she would be seen talking to herself or talking to a tree, a squirrel, or if someone was walking a dog, she would stop them and have a conversation with the dog, disregarding the person.

Somehow, luckily for her, the disability was approved, and they awarded her enough to live on, able to feed herself and her four cats.

She was not at all what you would call a clean person. If you opened her apartment door, you would immediately get hit with the smell of cats, kitty litter, old bowls that had been in the sink for who knows how long, and just a very underlying stench of mothballs. Not a pungent smell, but it was enough to be able to sense it standing in her doorway.

Her sink was full of dirty dishes, last week's macaroni and cheese plastered to the side of the bowls, now looking like hard, white plastic pieces of dried pasta. If you walked by, put your ear to the door, and listened, you would hear the sounds of silverware falling onto the floor, the sounds of pots and pans clanging together or falling on the floor because her cats, often underfed, had jumped up into the sink, hoping to get traces of last night's (*or last week's*) leftovers.

Her apartment was full of end of times books. She could recite the book of Revelation backward, and she would always go on and on about life after death and how the world would end. To put it nicely, she was what everyone would call *nuts*. She named her furniture; she'd let bugs crawl all over the floor and walls (because it was wrong to kill them) and would usually shower about every fifth or sixth day.

Her dramatic outburst at the gas station yesterday was not unusual to those who knew her. In fact, she had almost had the police called on her before at this same gas station because they sold cigarettes (that was a story in itself) and she had been banned from the grocery store across the street. The problem is, this little tirade she went on yesterday was the first time she was speaking truth and making any real sense. But, just like the boy who cried wolf, people stopped listening long ago.

It started two nights ago. She was lying on the couch, the TV on a late-night local religious station that would usually play old church services, show old gospel choirs clapping and sweating in unison, and show an occasional Lawrence Welk rerun. On that night, as she lay there sleeping, the light from the TV flashing off the walls and reflecting off of her glasses, she immediately jolted upright, thinking someone was knocking at her door. Sometimes it is hard to tell here, in this apartment complex, if someone is knocking on your door or your neighbor's door. She slowly got up, a low, inaudible sermon coming from the TV speakers, where a morbidly obese pastor was going on and on about Job from the Old Testament. She put her feet on the floor, finally getting the nerve to creep to her door and look out the peephole to see what she could see. She took off her glasses, shut her right eye, and put her wide-open left eye to the hole. *Nothing.* She carefully opened the door, thinking she would have the element of surprise if someone was standing there. She poked her head out to see a lot more nothingness. *Dark.* She could faintly hear the light to the entryway buzzing as a few bugs swirled around it.

She came back into the living room, where the pastor on the TV in a gray suit was now holding up a Bible in his right hand. She turned on the kitchen light, grabbed a glass jug out of the refrigerator, and poured herself a glass of tea. She poured a small amount into a glass, spilling some on the kitchen floor. She wiped it up with the sock she was wearing, her left foot going in a back-and-forth movement, like a baseball player walking up to home plate, digging in before he takes his stance. She popped a nerve pill, making a grimacing face as she swallowed, then returned to her chair. Two of her cats, one white and black, the other all black, jumped up and started purring beside her. Cat hair riddled the back of the couch.

She smiled as she finished the rest of her tea and motioned to set the glass down on her coffee table, not having much luck finding a place because it was littered with mail, old newspapers, and old magazines. She was drifting off to sleep, now the TV showing an infomercial for a colon cleanser, when a flash of light outside came through her side door and caught her eye. Curiously, she got up to investigate, half asleep, slowly feeling the nerve medication taking the edge off.

She rubbed her eyes, unsure of what she was seeing, her vision adjusting to the darkness. Four apartments down, a very tall man was pacing back and forth between a side window and a side door, looking in. She instantly thought about the Bible, and how this pervert, a peeping tom she had caught in the act, would one day have to repent of his sins and answer for his actions here on earth. It made her radically nut job religious heart happy to think about someone paying for their sins.

They'll all pay one day.

The night was so dark that she had a hard time seeing what this guy was doing. Her view was partially obstructed by one neighbor's grill and patio furniture and another neighbor's porch light that hung just perfectly in her line of sight. The dark figure looked like he was trying to see if anyone was home or was trying to follow a person walking around in their apartment. Voyeurism at its finest.

He stood there, looking in the side window for what seemed like an hour, but was more like five or ten minutes, when the sound of plastic tupperware hit the kitchen floor behind her, and she jumped. One of her cats, desperately looking for a drink of water and a scrap of food, had knocked it off of the kitchen counter. She inhaled sharply and turned around. She walked over, picked up the empty bowl, turned on the kitchen sink, and filled it with water. She placed it on the kitchen floor, and all four cats raced toward it like they hadn't had water for days (*three or four days, maybe. Maybe longer*).

Sandy, half scared, half excited to catch someone committing such a horrible sin, walked back to the window. Adrenaline coursed through her; she could feel the electricity in the heels of her feet. She was grinning like a villain when she peered outside her sliding glass door. No one was there now. Across the street, she saw another man (*or was it the same one?*) walking through the parking lot towards another side window. This man did the same thing. He paced back and forth, peering through windows creepily, she assumed, hoping to catch a glimpse of a woman undressing. What happened next, she wasn't sure if she could explain. The man put his hands on the wall of the apartment and disappeared. At least, that's what she thought she saw. Her eyes weren't as good as they once were, and when her nerve pills were on board, sometimes reality was a little distorted.

Her reality was always distorted.

She stood there waiting for a few minutes, no thoughts of calling the police, only thoughts of the afterlife and this man or these men, having to explain to God himself why they were spying on people in the middle of the night.

A few actionless minutes passed. Her eyes started to roll in the back of her head. She turned around for another night of self-medicated induced sleep when the man, who she thought had to be almost ten feet tall, appeared again outside of the side window of the apartment across the street. She watched him move again, while she donned an expression like an old teacher who was making a student confess to something they had done. The man turned, this time heading back to the parking lot, headed for the wooded area on the east side of the complex.

Next to the pond.

"I see you. You're not fooling me. God is watching you, too. Heathen," she whispered, hatefully, with a slight arrogance.

As the judgmental words left her lips, the man slowly turned around as if he had heard her. She took a step back, almost falling over her coffee table. A stack of old magazines fell over and spilled onto the floor. The man looked in her direction. She couldn't tell for sure, but he looked like he was smiling. Large, deathly yellow eyes met hers. She had never seen anything like it. She grabbed her Bible off of the kitchen table, and it shook in her trembling hands. She prayed, knowing the Lord would save her.

CHAPTER 20

"Alright, you losers have stolen enough money from me tonight," Dave said as he glanced up at the clock on his bedroom wall. He raised his arms over his head, stretching, inhaling as he did so. He wasn't surprised when he realized he had been playing online poker for just over three and a half hours. As he yawned, he pushed back from his desk, and his chair moved backward with a creak.

His bedroom contained a never made queen-sized bed, his computer desk that he had picked up from someone's yard, where a white sign that read *"free"* hung off one side, one single lamp with a tan-colored lamp shade covered in cobwebs and dead insects on the inside, a nightstand that had four old cups he never returned to the kitchen sink, a flat-screen TV with wires coming out from every direction, and dirty clothes on the floor, flung everywhere like piles of Legos a child had dumped out of a toy bin.

Dave walked into the kitchen, scratching his butt as he walked. He flicked on the light, and his eyes squinted to adjust to the brightness. He yawned, opening the refrigerator door, then moved the Chinese carry-out he had from five nights ago, still in its white carton with red Chinese letters on the side, and grabbed the half-gallon of milk.

He opened, then sniffed it, taking a big gulp directly from the carton. The expiration date was two days ago, but that didn't seem to bother Dave Langley in the least bit. He closed the carton, milk still swishing around in his mouth. He let out a burp as he opened the refrigerator door and placed the milk back inside. For a second, he thought about grabbing the Chinese food and having a midnight snack, reaching for it but changing his mind at the same time.

Dave walked back into his bedroom and sat down on his bed. He removed his socks, one by one, throwing them on the floor, letting them blend in with the other dirty clothes. He picked up his phone and set an alarm for 6:30 the next morning. Dave had already decided that he would call in sick tomorrow if he felt too tired to go to work. He still had four sick days he could use by the end of December, and a Monday morning seemed like as good a time as any to use one.

He fell asleep in his t-shirt and boxers, his bulging, pale stomach peeking out like a half-moon. As he lay there, semi-covered by a red blanket, his white sheet rolled up into a ball at the back of his knees, he dreamt about a life that could have been.

He dreamed it was his wedding day. His bride, someone he had never seen before, with long, beautiful dark hair, smiled at him as she sauntered down the aisle towards her groom-to-be.

His children were there, sitting in the front row, beaming with pride, ecstatic their dad had finally gotten his life together. He had, in this dream, become more involved in their life, everyone in the Langley family finally where they all should be. Fidgety and sweating, he looked down at his daughter. She smiled and mouthed *"I love you"* to him. That made him feel calm and at ease. He felt tears of joy form in the corner of his eyes. He knew he couldn't look back down at her, or he would lose it. He tried to think about anything else.

I love my baby girl.

His bride-to-be stepped in front of him, still smiling, and removed the veil from her face. He had never felt so happy as he let out a breath of air to relax and smiled back at her, looking directly into her eyes. She took another step and reached out to him. Her hand, small and gentle, connected to an arm, tan with smooth skin. As she reached up to touch his face, Dave jerked awake.

He was soaked in sweat, and his heart was beating rapidly. He had a multitude of feelings pirouetting through his system. The dream, which seemed like had lasted thirty seconds, caused Dave to think about his life. He had not been the father he knew he could be. He knew he had not been the husband he should have been, either. To *both* wives. He felt his throat slowly close up as a tear ran down his left cheek.

Dave pushed himself up with one arm, and he sat on the edge of his bed. Sorrow inundated him as he put his glasses on and looked up at the clock. He was in disbelief that he had been asleep for almost three hours. It was 3:15 am.

As he sat there, chin resting in his palms, he felt a sense of hope for his future. He couldn't help but think that the dream had some type of psychic meaning. Maybe some hopeful foreshadowing events to come.

Thinking about his children, he imagined the future. He decided he would call them tomorrow and apologize for everything over the years. Dave made a promise to himself that he would change. He would be the man he knew he should be. It would start here, now, on the edge of this bed. He never thought about marrying again, but maybe, he hoped, this change would offer him a new life with a clean slate.

He licked his lips, desperately needing a drink of water. He looked over at his nightstand, now disgusted with himself, seeing all the dirty glasses. He scooped them all up, then stepped over his dirty clothes and headed down the hall towards the kitchen.

The light came on as the switch clicked, and he placed the dirty glasses in the sink carefully, as if he were trying not to wake anyone up. He opened the cabinet and grabbed a blue plastic cup that had faded white letters on the side from years of being washed. He turned on the sink, held the cup under the cold running water, and filled it.

Something is in here.

Beings had one thing they couldn't hide. Regardless of what form they'd taken on, their reflection in a mirror or window would always reveal their dark green skin and yellow eyes in their true form. A weakness? Perhaps their only weakness.

This one, which had followed him quietly down the hall as he went to get a drink of water, could take on the form of his two neighbors, Steve and Andrea Williams, who lived next door. Earlier tonight, as they watched TV in bed, they were both overpowered and taken over. Andrea's face full of sheer terror as it happened.

Go to sleep, little darling.

Dave did not notice the yellow eyes behind him staring at him in the window's reflection as he drank the water. The *Being* behind him didn't try to hide it, either, knowing he already had the element of surprise. Dave sniffed and frowned. A bitter odor entered his nostrils.

As the dark green hand reached out for the top of Dave's head, he turned around just at the right time, and the B*eing's* hand clipped the side of his face and shoulder. He gasped as he dropped the plastic cup, spilling water on the floor. The blue cup bounced with a *smack*, then rolled into the living room.

Unsure of what he was looking at, his mind in shock, Dave backed away slowly. The thing, whatever it was, moved towards him. The yellow eyes were looking into Dave's, and the creature seemed to smile.

Why do they always seem to smile?

"What…what are you?" Dave said to it like it would answer him. The thing, still seeming to smile, moved closer to him and raised its hands, its body towering over his.

As quickly as he could, Dave threw one of his dining room chairs into the path of the thing and ran towards the cabinet to grab a knife. He grabbed the first one his trembling hand could find and turned to face the giant creature, as if they were about to duel in a sword fight.

The *Being* took a step towards Dave, and Dave swiped at it with his knife, missing. The thing raised its hands and opened its mouth, showing a long, red snake-like tongue. Dave swiped at it again, missing and losing his balance.

The thing raised its hand, and Dave watched in shock as it lifted its index finger, revealing a claw the size of a four-inch blade.

Returning the favor, it swung its arm in a stabbing motion, missing, and Dave fell against his kitchen counter, his feet slipping in the spilled water as he crashed to the floor. Dave's knife slid across the floor, coming to rest against the dining room chair he had turned on its side. The massive hand reached for him. It grabbed Dave by the throat and lifted him in the air. Dave could smell it, a stench of mildew mixed with something that had started to rot.

Dave's kicking feet slowed as he lost consciousness. He was thinking about his kids, and an eerie, quiet calmness overcame him. The four-inch blade plunged into his chest with a crack, and Dave's body went limp and lifeless.

The thing, still wearing something on its face that resembles a smile, dropped Dave's body on the floor into a pool of his own blood.

CHAPTER 21

Garrett's alarm buzzed, but he had been awake for almost thirty minutes. He could barely sleep last night. He was excited to call his parents, to give them all the details, knowing they'd be bursting with happiness. He told himself he would call them on the way home from work later that day.

After his prosaic morning routine and the same dull drive to the BelTech parking lot, Garrett parked, grabbed his bag, hopped out of his car and walked toward the entrance. He had a little more pep in his step on this warm Monday morning.

As he entered the building with his ID badge, he told himself to keep calm. He was worried a date with Laura would make things awkward for him here, in these four walls, like they had secretly been hiding an affair from the rest of their coworkers. He closed his eyes and hoped things hadn't changed between them, worried everyone already knew somehow, anyway.

Smiling at every BelTech employee he passed, his ID badge bouncing off his leg with every bend of the knee, he turned the corner where two women were whispering about another employee and saw Laura taking a drink of coffee at her desk. He smiled as their eyes met, and his anxiety morphed into relief. There was a difference in the smile, for sure, but the way she did it told him they were still just coworkers inside this building.

I'm good with that.

Garrett made his way to his desk, setting his bag down. His mind had been so fixated on his date (and Laura's legs) that he realized he left his water bottle on his kitchen counter. He was sheepishly glad he forgot it. It gave him another excuse to pass Laura's office once more to get a cup at the water cooler at the end of the hall, next to the two gossipers.

He passed her office again; her smile was a little more seductive this time, and his mind went to their kiss again. He wanted another. He filled up his cup, made eye contact with her, and walked back to his desk, his mind still wandering on and on.

Garrett looked at Dave's empty chair, then turned around to look at the clock that hung above his desk. It was unusual for Dave to not be in already. He was usually the first in their area to get in, thinking it would mean he could be the first one out the door when it came time to leave. Garrett paused for a moment, forming an expression of concentration.

Is Dave off today?

He plugged in his laptop to check his calendar to see if Dave had a vacation or personal day requested. Besides a few afternoon meetings, there was nothing.

He dropped it for now and started on a project that had been thrown on him last minute. His boss, never one to have much consideration for his employee's time, threw this on Garrett's already full plate this morning. It's a double-edged sword when you're an employee that people can trust and count on. You get more work thrown on you without more pay, because you work with people who are lazy assholes. Seems fair.

An hour and a half passed on the clock while Garrett was nose-deep into his new assignment. Sports radio was coming through his computer speakers as he focused on the screen.

"Where's Langley?" A voice almost shouted in his ear.

He half jumped as if he had been startled from a dream. "I was actually going to ask you the same thing," Garrett said to his boss.

James Martin, Garrett's boss, was leaning over the half wall of Garrett's cubicle, arms crossed. James had been at BelTech for nearly ten years now and had been Garrett's manager for the last two.

"What do you mean?" James asked, frowning.

"I hadn't heard from him, so I thought maybe he called in sick or had a vacation day I forgot about," Garrett said, turning around in his chair.

"Not that I'm aware of. I haven't heard from him, either," James said as he turned toward Dave's empty chair.

"Should I try to call him?" Garrett asked, now concerned something had happened.

James shrugged his shoulders and said, "I suppose it wouldn't hurt." He paused for a few seconds and then added, "Yeah, give him a call, just to check."

Garrett pulled out his phone, remembering at the same time he needed to call his parents on his way home from work. He scrolled through, finding Dave's contact info. He pushed the button on the screen to call. Garrett sat, swiveling back and forth in his chair, the phone held up to his ear. After the seventh ring, it went to voicemail, and he looked up at James, now feeling worried about his coworker.

Dave had been dead for almost eight hours.

"No answer," Garrett said, putting the phone down on his desk.

James adjusted his belt. "We can try later. Maybe he's sick and forgot to call in. He could still be asleep in bed."

"Yeah. I will try him later," Garrett said, but still feeling like something was off. He sat more upright, grabbing his phone. "I'll shoot him a text," Garrett said, typing away on his phone keyboard.

This isn't like him.

"Let me know if you hear from him. Hey, that thing I sent you this morning," James said, walking backward, staring at Garrett. "Let me have your rough draft by Thursday afternoon, please."

"No problem," Garrett said, uninterested, looking back down at his phone. He settled back in, took a drink of water, and got back to work. He looked back down at his phone, waiting for a reply that would never come.

Hunger came out of nowhere, and Garrett headed down to Suzie's. He passed by Laura's office and noticed it was empty. Gaining a little enthusiasm, he walked faster to the cafeteria, expecting to see her there. He wanted to sit with her, and he didn't care if people saw. They were just friends. Coworkers with what Garrett felt like was a deceitful secret, but he loved that feeling.

The different salads, placed out for people to grab, did not look the least bit appetizing to Garrett. Instead, he passed a few people in line and walked down by the sign that read, "Hot Plate."

"Can I get a grilled cheese?" Garrett asked the older lady wearing a black polo shirt and black hairnet.

The lady nodded without saying a word and disappeared into the back, where a younger guy with tattoos was flipping what looked like a sad attempt to be burgers.

Waiting, Garrett pulled out his phone, hoping to see a message from Dave. Still nothing. He briefly considered calling the police but didn't want to jump to conclusions. It was Dave, after all.

Relax, he's fine. He's probably asleep in bed.

Or suffering from a hangover from an all-nighter of online poker.

The grilled cheese came slightly burned, and Garrett had also asked for a pickle spear on the side. He grabbed water out of the small refrigerator-looking case and paid for his meal. There was a seat at an empty table in the corner where someone had spilled salt. He blew it on the floor as he sat down, setting everything down on the now clean table.

As he sat, thinking about Laura, Dave, his project, and the Detroit Tigers, crunching on a grilled cheese that somehow still tasted like perfection, his phone dinged with a notification. It was Laura.

"I was going to text you earlier to see if you wanted to meet in the cafeteria, but a few of us from HR went out for lunch," her message read, the mystery of her whereabouts now solved.

"No worries. I guess I will have to eat my grilled cheese all alone," he typed back. He still felt like he was taking a big risk and the thought of having an office romance that he had to keep quiet excited him.

She responded with a smiley face emoji. After a few seconds, she wrote again, *"Can I call you tonight?"*

Garrett, now with a stupid grin on his face, held up his phone and typed back. *"Please do."*

Another smiley face emoji appeared on his phone as he bit into his pickle. He looked around, feeling like a teenager who had a secret he couldn't wait to let out.

After lunch, Garrett sat back at his desk, a full, sleepy belly now on board, working away and listening to sports radio. It was as quiet as an afternoon as he could remember. He checked his phone again and then turned around to look at Dave's empty chair and desk, his absence still not sitting right with him.

He got up, pushed his chair back in, and walked to James' office. James sat there, in his high and mighty manager chair, glasses pulled down to the bridge of his nose, reading something but mouthing it with his lips. Garrett knocked on the door, and James motioned for him to enter.

"Hey, sorry to bother," Garrett said with his hands in his pockets. "I just don't feel right about Dave. I've tried to call and text, and he hasn't responded. Do you think we should call the police?"

James took his glasses off and set them down on his desk. "Well, I'd hate to cause a panic if it's nothing, but it is unlike him not to call or respond."

"I'll call," Garrett said, pulling out his phone.

"Shut my door, will you?" James said. "I don't want anyone to worry over nothing."

Garrett held the phone to his ear as it rang.

"911, what's your emergency?" a lady's voice said into Garrett's ear.

"Hi, my name is Garrett Bradley. I am an employee at BelTech. A coworker of mine never showed up today, and he isn't responding to calls or texts. I was hoping to see if anyone could go check on him?"

"And what is the employee's name?" the lady on the other end said.

"His name is Dave Langley. He is probably mid-forties," Dave said, unsure why he gave her Dave's age.

"What is the address of your coworker, sir?"

"Uhhh, good question. I didn't even think of getting that," Garrett said, walking over to James' desk. He took the phone away from his ear and said in a half-whisper, "Can you get Dave's address real quick?"

James started typing on his computer. "Just a sec," he said and put his glasses on again. After a few clicks of the keyboard, he said, "Here it is," and looked up to Garrett. "It's 10660 Quail Run Circle, Apartment 2G. Millersville, MI."

Garrett repeated the address into the phone, now pacing in the middle of the office.

"We will send someone over right away. Thank you," the lady said and hung up before Garrett had a chance to respond.

"It's probably nothing, but I feel a little better knowing it'll get checked out," Garrett said to James as he put his phone back in his pocket.

"You're right, probably nothing at all," James said. Garrett knew his boss well enough to notice the look of worry he had on his face.

His phone rang, and James looked up at Garrett.

"Excuse me," he said to Garrett, picking up the phone. He gave a light-hearted wave, walked out of James' office, and shut the door.

Garrett walked back to his desk to continue working on his project. He plopped down in his chair, thinking about Dave. "I'm sure it's nothing," he said under his breath.

CHAPTER 22

Garrett spent the rest of the afternoon working on his newly assigned project, listening to sports radio, and worrying about Dave. He wondered if the police would call them back, giving them an update that they had found Dave snoring in bed, covered in empty wrappers and chip crumbs. They could laugh about it tomorrow.

At 4:30, he closed his laptop and began packing his things. He stood up, pushed his chair in, and threw his bag over his left shoulder. He turned the corner and headed down the hall. Another day of IT security down.

He passed Laura's office as she was straightening a stack of papers on her desk. He knocked on the propped-open door and entered. She looked up at him, surprised, with welcoming eyes.

"How was lunch?" he said, mostly flirting.

"It was good. I'm sure it wasn't as good as your grilled cheese," she said, smiling.

"Black grilled cheese," he said with a grin. "They torched it pretty good. Still not bad."

"Well, I'm glad it was still good," she said, feelings for him growing by the minute.

"Are you walking out?" He asked, hoping she was, so they could walk out together.

"Unfortunately, not. I have to meet with Rita for a minute. Can I still call you tonight?" she asked as she pulled her hair back behind her ear.

"Yes. Yes. Please do. I should be free all night," he said and moved his bag to his other shoulder.

"I will," she said and smiled. They both stood there, unsure of what to say next.

"Okay then. Call me," he said, turning around to see if anyone had heard. No one was around.

Secret is safe.

"Okay then," she said, laughing. She opened a desk drawer and placed some papers inside.

A few seconds of awkward silence passed.

"Well, have a good night," Garrett said as he started for the door.

"You, too," she said, still working with her stack of papers.

Garrett's black car headed west, merging onto the interstate, blending in with the flow of traffic. He pushed the phone button on the dashboard and tapped his parents' contact info, ready to give them all the details he figured they had been waiting all day to hear. The phone rang as he turned on his turn signal and entered the left lane.

He sped up as the phone rang. It rang several times. He hit the red button on the steering wheel, ending the call. Garrett grabbed his sunglasses out of the middle console and placed them over his eyes, assuming his parents were at the store, outside doing yard work, or sitting on their porch. His mind shifted to Laura, and he swallowed. Part of him wanted her to call now.

Getting closer to the exit, his pace slowed to an almost crawl, all the cars trying to get over to the far right line to exit to Burnley. He made his way over without issue and continued the drive he had made a million times.

He pulled into his driveway, the sun turning from a bright ball of orange to a more faded late afternoon yellow. It wasn't as hot as the forecast had called for, settling into a comfortable high seventies, much better than the low nineties the guy in the suit on TV had promised.

Garrett put the car in park.

No one outside again.

He walked inside, throwing his computer bag onto the kitchen table, noticing the water bottle sitting on the counter he had forgotten earlier. He pursed his lips at his forgetfulness. He bent over and lifted his legs, one by one, removing his shoes from each foot. He grabbed the water and fell into the couch with an exhale, held up the remote, and turned on the TV.

He turned on the news, which seemed to be anything but good news these days, lately wondering why he even continued watching anymore. The pessimistic stories only seemed to fill him with depression.

Tonight, though, there was a story of an elderly woman who was retiring from the local zoo, being thanked for her years of dedicated service. She had been the longest-tenured employee the zoo had, retiring after fifty-six years. Garrett smiled as he watched. The story was sweet and light-hearted, and it made him think about calling his parents.

He grabbed his phone, tapped a few times on the screen, and the phone rang in his ear. He sat on the edge of the couch, looking outside, the TV now showing a graph depicting obesity in the United States.

Ahh, and now to our depressing, developing story.

No answer. He tapped the screen again and frowned as he locked his phone. He set it down on the coffee table and cracked his neck.

He made himself a turkey sandwich with two pieces of turkey and a piece of swiss cheese, covering them both in mayonnaise and mustard. He ripped off a piece of paper towel for a napkin, grabbed his sandwich he had put on a paper plate, and headed back for the comfort of the couch. His phone rang as he sat down, displaying a number he didn't recognize. He picked it up and tapped the green button on the screen.

"Hello?" he said, annoyed.

There was nothing on the other end. Garrett waited about four or five seconds and hung up.

Not even going to ask me about my car's extended warranty?

He placed the phone down on the table and continued watching the news.

He ate his sandwich, not really interested, but it was enough to keep him full for the night. He got up to throw his trash away, thinking about going for a jog, knowing he needed to get some type of exercise in today. He opened the trash with his foot, balancing on the other, then let the lid shut with a thud. His phone rang again.

It was Laura. He coughed out loud to clear his throat.

"Hey there," he said, trying to sound relaxed.

Don't sound too eager.

"Hi!" she said, not trying to hide the excitement. "Sorry I couldn't talk earlier. Rita was pissed about something."

"Isn't she always pissed about something?" Garrett said, and he meant it.

"She is. She's really not that bad, though," Laura said, almost sounding defensive.

"Every time I see her, she looks like she hates the world," Garrett said into the phone. He picked at his teeth.

"She's just insanely serious about her job. I don't know why. You know how some people just love their job? Well, she's one of them. She lives and breathes the world of human resources."

"Sounds like a good life," Garrett said. "Maybe I should ask her out to an Italian restaurant."

"Hey now!" She almost yelled into the phone. "I think we should just keep this between us."

Garrett felt sixteen again. "That's fine with me. She's not really my type, anyway."

"Oh? What is your type?" Laura asked flirtatiously.

"I like HR girls, but not like Rita. I like them a little younger, with dark hair. Named Laura," he said, the words pouring out without control.

Easy, killer. Don't scare her off.

"Good. Because you have one just like that." He could hear a slight tremble in her voice.

"That's good to hear," he said. "Maybe we should plan something for this weekend. We could go out, or you could come here. I'm really open to anything. I will let you decide. What do you think? Are you ok with that? Are you free this coming weekend?"

There was no answer. He paused for a second, worried he had crossed the line.

Not just crossed it, bulldozed over it.

"Oh my God," she almost whispered into the phone.

"What? What's wrong?" Garrett said as he sat up straight. He was rigid.

"Are you watching the news?" she said, and he felt a little relieved.

"I had it on earlier, but I haven't really been watching," he said; the screen he was watching was now showing a commercial for hair loss.

"They found four people murdered in an apartment building on the east side of town. Looks like someone broke into a few apartments, but they aren't really releasing much detail. Must mean they don't really have anything yet," she said. Her mind was racing.

Garrett turned the channel to another local news station and saw the same story Laura was watching. He could hear her television in the background, hers a few words ahead of his, and he wondered how that sometimes happened. His stomach dropped as he saw the images on the screen. It was Dave's apartment complex.

CHAPTER 23

Garrett had told Laura he was going to try Dave's number one more time, not sounding hopeful. She was sad the conversation was ending so abruptly, but she understood. They said their goodbyes, and she made herself a bowl of leftover chicken and noodle soup.

After dinner, she cuddled with a purple and white blanket she had had since high school. The ends had frayed, showing the usual wear and tear all blankets that people can't seem to get rid of, show. She flipped through the DVR and found the latest episode of a reality show where plastic blonde bimbos, who have been surgically Frankensteined into models, gossip about each other and sell houses. In it, they sell houses and work all day, go out for lunch and dinner, and never have to watch their kids.

She yawned, uninterested in the episode, and picked up her phone. She scrolled through her social media, "liking" a few posts, laughing at a few videos where cats fell off couches.

A post her friend had shared caught her attention, and she muted the television as she read it. The post, which had been shared over nine hundred times now, was posted to an "Everything Central Michigan" page. The post had an apocalyptic message. She was sure some whackjob had written it trying to get attention. It read like a joke in which she didn't know the punchline.

The post had originated from a blogger named "FarmLivin2005."

The post read, "Citizens of Central Michigan-We know they are here. We have seen them. We have transformed the cafeteria of the old LBD building downtown into a safe haven. We have food, we have water, we have medicine. Please grab your loved ones and join us. We are expecting you."

Laura leaned forward, a furrowed brow causing creases around her eyes. She read through the comments, trying to decipher the message. Was this a joke? There had been nothing on the news tonight about this. Someone was playing an elaborate hoax, and they were playing it well. She counted at least twenty comments where someone had messaged that they were there or were headed there.

The old LBD building (Lintner, Barton, and Darrows) had been a plastics factory that shut down nearly ten years ago and had sat abandoned, with graffiti now decorating the outsides in colorful, artistic patterns. There had been several plans to demolish, and at one point, there were plans for it to become an outpatient surgery center. Plans that had obviously fallen through.

Laura, now curious, looked up other social media posts that were similar. She searched for other posts like the one she had just read. She typed "LBD Plastics" and "Downtown" in her search. One result showed pictures of families sitting together and smiling. There were images of kids playing together, people eating together, some with white blankets over their shoulders.

The comment section read like an end-of-times cult message board. She kept scrolling. "We are finally safe here from them," one post read. Another, "My family and I were attacked, but we all survived. Everyone here at the LBD building took us in, and now we feel completely safe."

Skepticism led to curiosity, curiosity led to intrigue, and now Laura was rounding second base, heading for third, which was fear. If this wasn't real, someone had done an immaculate job pulling off the hoax of the century. She went back to watching the news.

A knock on the door made Laura jump, and her phone crashed down on the floor. She got up, half-folded her blanket, and placed her phone on the coffee table. She walked up to her front window, brushed the curtain to the side with one hand, and looked out at her porch. Her neighbor, Shannon Collins, was standing on her front porch, cigarette in hand.

Laura opened the door, instantly hit in the face with cigarette smoke. She smiled at Shannon.

"Hey, Shannon," Laura said to her.

"Hey there. I am sorry to bother you, but do you have a cup of sugar I can borrow?" Shannon asked, smiling, blowing smoke into the air.

"Umm, yeah, I think-"

"I'm kidding. I know you went on a date last night, and I want to hear all about it," Shannon said.

"Oh," Laura said, laughing. "You're crazy. I was standing here debating with myself if I even had sugar."

Laura and Shannon had been friends for over a year now, as long as Laura has lived in the condo. Shannon, now divorced, had one adult daughter who lived in New York City. At least once a week, Shannon and Laura would sit out on her front porch and talk about the latest celebrity news or show they'd been watching. Laura loved having her around as a mother figure, her own mother now living in Cleveland, where her father moved them when he started his own consulting firm when Laura graduated from college.

"So tell me about him," Shannon said, her cigarette now out but still held between her index and middle fingers.

"Well, I work with him. He's adorable. He's never been married. No kids."

"Does he make good money?" Shannon asked and coughed into her fisted hand.

"He does well, yes. He's incredibly smart, too. Not like dorky smart. Smart like…like everyone at work goes to him when they need something done. He's just…like perfect," Laura said, her smile not concealed.

"Did you...I mean, did he come in last night?" Shannon asked like they were teenagers the day after prom.

"No!" Laura said defensively. "Not on a first date."

"Well, I'm just asking. Us old ladies still like to know the details, honey," Shannon said and grabbed on to the railing.

Laura knew Shannon spent a majority of her time reading online news and scrolling through social media. It made her think of the post she was reading twenty minutes ago.

"Hey, let me ask you something," Laura said, her face looking more serious now. "Have you read anything online about people going to the old LBD building downtown for a safe haven?"

"Safe haven? For what?" She shook her head. "I haven't seen anything," Shannon said and grabbed another cigarette.

"I'm not really sure. There was a post, and it said something along the lines of people had seen *them* and they would be safe if they came downtown to that building. It even said they had food and water and medicine or something like that."

Shannon blew a cloud of smoke into the air and waved it with her hand. "Not that I have seen. And what do they mean by *them*?"

Laura shrugged.

"That's really weird. It's either something fake, or it's some kind of cult. Don't believe everything you read, dear," Shannon said and coughed a raspy smoker's cough.

"Yeah, that's what I thought, too, but I don't know. It was weird. It sort of freaked me out a little," Laura said with a worried look on her face. She moved to the side to avoid the smoke lingering in front of her.

Laura showed Shannon the post, showed her the pictures, read the comments out loud, and the conversation shifted back to Garrett, which was the gossip Shannon came for in the first place.

Shannon lit up another cigarette and walked back to her porch. She finished and flicked it, the orange glow going end over end in the air. It started to rain.

CHAPTER 24

When Garrett arrived at his desk Tuesday morning, his boss was waiting for him, sitting in his seat. James had an uncomfortable look on his face. Garrett sat his bag and water on the desk, trying to read James Martin's eyes. Whatever it was, it wasn't good.

Don't tell me it's Dave.

"What's going on?" Garrett said, feeling like he already knew the answer.

"Let's go to my office, real quick. I need to talk with you about something," James said, standing up. He held his glasses up to the light and wiped them off in his shirt, squinting as he did so.

"What is it?" Garrett said, his mind now racing as James started toward his office.

James didn't answer.

"Hey," Garrett said, grabbing James' arm. "What's going on? Tell me."

"It's Dave," James said. His voice was almost a whisper. He looked around to see if anyone was listening. "Let's go to my office," he said, his voice low and intentional.

The two men walked into James' office. The lights, which turn on with movement, blasted on. Garrett thought they seemed brighter today. James let Garrett move past him, then shut the door. The color had run out of his face.

Please don't.

"We received a call from the police department this morning," James said. He sat down at his desk and placed his glasses carefully next to his keyboard. Garrett noticed a slight tremble in his lips. James rubbed his eyes and continued, "Dave was killed last night, Garrett. I don't know how, or why, and that's all the information we were given. His family knows, obviously. I know, and HR knows. They are working on it now, but we are going to call an impromptu staff meeting at some point to inform everyone."

Garrett leaned up against the wall and slid down, then sat on the floor. A mix of grief and nausea coursed through him. He put his hands on his knees and his head back against the wall.

James stood up and went over to him. "I'm sorry, Garrett. I know you two were friends. I'm just as shocked as you. If you need to take the day off to go home to deal with this, I completely understand. Please, take the day if you need it," James said, bending over toward Garrett, his hand resting on Garrett's left shoulder.

"No. No, thanks. I think I will be ok. I just can't believe this. I'm just….in shock."

"I understand. As am I. You never think this sort of thing will happen to someone you know. This is a first for me as a manager," James said, standing up and looking out his office window.

"I think I need a drink of water and to step outside for a minute. Get a little fresh air," Garrett said, standing up.

"Take all the time you need. And if you feel like you need to, please take the day, Garrett. I know this is not an easy thing to work through," James said sympathetically. His face was gentle and understanding.

Garrett, standing but still leaning against the wall, rubbed his forehead and looked at James. "I appreciate you letting me know. I think I am okay, but I just want some air," Garrett said, now looking down at the floor.

"Understand," James replied. "And I'll be here if you need to come chat."

"Thanks," Garrett said. He stood there for another few seconds with a blank expression on his face. He turned toward the door and left the room. He headed for his desk, but turned, desperately hoping not to run into anyone and have to make small talk, pretending he hadn't just had a nuclear bomb dropped on him. His feet led him in the opposite direction.

He turned left, passing the restrooms on the left and the small break room on the right. He continued head down to the ground, looking at the gray carpet. Straight ahead, behind the brown wooden door under the green exit sign, were the stairs that led outside. He went down the stairs as fast as he could, his ID badge flying like a water hose out of control.

Garrett walked outside, thinking of Dave and his family. He walked through some mulch that smelled new toward the side of the parking lot, where picnic tables were placed neatly in rows by a column of evergreen trees. He walked to the last one and sat on top of it. It creaked. Garrett put his hands down and felt the rough wood, the sun keeping it a comfortable warm that felt good on his palms. An ant crawled on his hand, and he flung it off. He felt nauseous again.

The urge to call his parents overtook him. He slapped the side of his leg, frantically checking to see if his phone was in his pocket. He pulled it out as a group of birds flew over him. Their chirps, which usually sounded happy and inviting, appeared sad today as if they were joining Garrett in mourning.

He sat on the edge of the picnic table, his feet dangling below him. Garrett tapped the screen of his phone, then held it to his ear. He switched it to his other ear after the first ring. They did not answer. Garrett tapped the screen.

With the news of Dave and a day and a half of no answer, Dave swiped on his screen and dialed 911. Again. He had never called 911, and now, in two days, he was calling them twice. He had a guilty feeling as if he were wasting someone's time. This time, a younger man answered.

"911, what's your emergency?"

"Hi, this is Garrett Bradley." He paused, forgetting what he needed to say next. "I haven't been able to get in touch with my parents, which is very unlike them. I have a coworker, I *had* a coworker, he…he went missing…

No. He's dead, Garrett.

…so I guess I am just a little on edge right now. I need to see if someone can go check on them to make sure they are okay."

"What is their address, please? We can do a welfare check," the man said in a matter-of-fact way. He had probably answered this type of call a few thousand times, his voice coming over the phone with no emotion.

"It's 3081 E Terhune Drive, Waterton, Michigan. 49218," Garrett said, noticing a squirrel running up the tree beside him.

"We will have someone there right away, sir," the man said into the phone.

"Wait," Garrett said, interrupting him. "Will I be able to be notified?"

"We can not notify you, but if you have reason to believe they are in danger, you will have to call their local police department to speak to someone there. There is a non-emergency line you would have to dial to get in touch with someone there," the man said, sounding like he was reading from a script.

"I don't know why it has to be so hard! I could drive over there and have an answer faster than this," Garrett said, frustrated. He realized he was raising his voice.

"Is there anything else I can help with, sir?" The man said stoically.

"No. Thank you for your help," Garrett said, but not really meaning it. The call ended.

Garrett, starting to feel a little better, got up and headed back to the side stair entrance. The hum of a lawn mower was getting closer, echoing off the side of the building. A man in a straw hat passed him wearing an orange shirt. Garrett waved to him. The man paid no attention to Garrett, looking straight ahead, concentrating. He held his ID badge to the lock, the green light granting him access. He noticed his legs shaking as he walked upstairs.

He returned to his desk and turned on his computer. He took a drink of water and looked back at Dave's desk.

Hold it together.

There was a picture of Dave and his son, his son wearing a Cubs hat, probably six years old. Besides that one, there was one of Dave and his daughter at the zoo, both of them wearing hats with elephant trunks hanging down the front. Garrett choked back emotion, opening emails to distract him.

A notification came through that a staff meeting had been scheduled in an hour. Garrett accepted.

CHAPTER 25

The team gathered in the conference room, huddling around the large rectangular table. There was a bulky speaker that had four legs, looking like some type of insect from outer space, in the middle of the table with a BelTech logo on it. A small red light flashed on its side.

The team, unaware, made small talk, and one guy showed another a video on his phone. Most laughed while others checked their phones, oblivious to the macabre news they were about to receive and the emotions they would feel.

The conference room phone turned green, and remote employees were patched through.

James Martin walked in, a somber but serious look engraved on his face. He walked to the front of the room and leaned his arms on a small wooden podium. He sighed.

"Kelly, Nicole, anyone else on the phone, can you hear me?" he said, not looking up from the podium.

A plethora of voices came through the speaker. "Yes, we can hear you," they said.

"Okay, this is going to be a tough one. I wanted to bring everyone in here, to…umm…to, unfortunately, share some heartbreaking news," he said, his voice shaking. "We were informed by police this morning that Dave Langley passed away last night. Because of the ongoing investigation, unfortunately, I don't have any answers and don't know any details."

There was a collective gasp in the room. One older lady, Donna Sullivan, who used to sit by Dave, put her face in her hands and sobbed. Others sat and stared, not saying a word.

"Rita, will you let everyone know the next steps, please?" James said and moved away from the podium.

Rita Owens, who had been head of HR for a few years now, walked up to the podium wearing a pants suit. As horrible as a situation this was, it was more horrible how she reveled in it, enjoying the spotlight, trying to make things about her. She lived for these minutes where she could have the attention on her.

"This is a terrible tragedy, and it will, no doubt, affect us all in many different ways. We will have a grievance counselor on-site for the next two days if anyone feels they need help dealing with their emotions," she said, loving every minute of this. She continued, "Does anyone have any questions?"

The room was quiet, except for Donna Sullivan blowing her nose into a tissue. Someone's cell phone rang, and they stepped into the hall.

James Martin spoke up, "HR will be here as usual, all day, if anyone has any questions. I was thinking maybe tomorrow we could have a pitch in lunch or something to honor Dave," he said, the room a deafening quiet. Some people nodded, some stared at the floor, no one really acknowledging his statement.

Garrett stood up and walked up towards James.

"If I may just say a few words," Garrett said, looking uncomfortable. Laura looked up at him, her heart turning to putty.

He stood behind the podium, looking everyone in the eye before he spoke. "I knew Dave really well. We sat next to each other every day for a long time. He was a great friend and a great coworker. He had a way about him. I can't really explain it, but you just couldn't help but like him. Let's not forget that he was also a father, so we should all keep his family in your thoughts and prayers. I'm going to miss him, for sure. If we could, let's all take a minute or two in a moment of silence and just remember him," Garrett said, placing his hands on the podium and looking down.

The room went silent. Most bowed their heads, some sat looking forward, the shock not letting the news fully set in. Garrett's phone rang, and he picked it up to silence the call. It was a Waterton, Michigan phone number. He turned the volume down and jogged into the empty hall. He swiped to answer.

"Hello?" he said, with a hint of panic coming through in his voice.

"Hello, is this Garrett Bradley?" The man on the other end said.

"Yes, it is," Garrett said, and looked around, feeling the eerie silence in the hallway.

"Hello, Mr. Bradley. This is Shane Kirklin. I'm an officer with the Waterton police department."

Garrett's heart sank.

CHAPTER 26

"Is everything ok? Were you able to speak with my parents?" Garrett said, now quickly pacing down the hall toward his desk.

"Yes, sir. Everything is fine. Your dad answered the door, told us there was no trouble, and said maybe there was something wrong with his reception," Sheriff Kirklin said, as he crunched on a hand full of roasted nuts.

Garrett, ignoring the crunching in his ear, continued. "And he seemed perfectly fine? He's never really had any phone issues, so that just seems weird."

"Yeah, yeah. Everything checked out," the sheriff said and threw another handful into his mouth.

"Okay. Well, I will just try to call him later on today. Thank you for checking on them. I really appreciate it. And listen, sorry if it's a waste of time. I know there are bigger fish to fry, but I've been really worried, so thanks again," Garrett said. He didn't feel any better.

Something is off here.

"Yep. No problem. Call us anytime," Kirklin said into the phone. The call ended.

Everyone had started to filter out of the conference room, their faces full of sadness and grief. Garrett leaned against the wall, his coworkers giving him an *"I'm sorry"* look as they passed. Laura touched his arm as she went by, neither one caring if anyone saw. Garrett waited for James and walked back to his office with him.

Garrett spoke first. "If you don't mind, I might take the rest of the day. I want to go check on my parents and make sure they are okay."

"It's perfectly fine. I understand," James said, rubbing his temples. Garrett noticed the stress on his face, and he looked like he had aged a few years since yesterday. The wrinkles on his forehead seemed to run deeper than they had before.

"I appreciate it," Garrett said. He meant it. James was a very understanding boss who was great with people and led by example. At the moment, Garrett was thankful to have him as a manager. "Thank you."

James nodded.

Something had changed in Garrett over the last two days. Was it Dave's death, his feelings for Laura, or the struggle to contact his parents? He didn't know, but he noticed he was changing. He was starting to appreciate life in ways he hadn't before. He was noticing the little things we all do as we age and how certain life events can have effects on us that never make us see the world through the same lens we once did. Losing a family member, the birth of a child, falling in love, getting a divorce- these things all change us. Sometimes it's good, and sometimes it isn't, but the change comes, whether we want it to or not, like a good story where the words jump off a page and into your heart and urge you to do something different with your life and become a better version of yourself. The change comes, and maybe that's really where life begins for us, and we start to realize there's more to life than just satisfying our needs and trying to get everything we want. When we all realize we aren't invincible after all and that life really is as fragile as we never thought it was. And then the worst reality sets in, the one we all eventually come to hate. The reality that life goes by way too quickly. We are here for a minute and then gone in an instant. Life is a vapor, a mist. Whatever all that was and whatever it all meant, it was happening to Garrett now.

"You're welcome," James said, forcing a smile. "And Garrett, don't worry about that project for now. Have it to me by next Friday, and that'll be fine. It can wait."

"Thank you, James. I really appreciate it. And I am bad at this, but I realize I need to do a better job of this in my life, so I want to say thanks. Thanks for everything you've done for me here over the years," Garrett said sincerely. "I'll be in tomorrow at my usual time, ready to go."

James showed an appreciative smile and sat down in his chair.

It would be the last time Garrett Bradley ever saw James Martin.

CHAPTER 27

Garrett headed home to change clothes before going to his parents. He had several thoughts racing through his mind, a whirlwind of emotions carving through his brain like a deadly tornado. Mostly, he thought about Dave and how he wished he had some way to tell him goodbye. Another sickening realization of life pranced around in his head; we never know when the last time we see someone will be.

He arrived home, his neighborhood still an unusual kind of quiet, and raced inside to change into shorts and a shirt. He thought it might be a good idea to get his mother a cell phone, even though she had fought the idea for years.

He kicked off his shoes, walked down the hall, and entered his bedroom. He took off his khaki pants and blue BelTech polo, wadded them both up, then threw them on the floor. He grabbed a pair of shorts and a shirt, quickly putting them on, desperately wanting to check on his parents.

He sat down on the edge of his bed to change his socks. He stretched and stood up as the doorbell dinged, echoing through his house. He checked the alarm system on his phone. It was Brad Bayner.

He argued with himself for a split second, wanting to pretend he wasn't home, but his car in the driveway gave that little secret away. He opened the door.

"Brad, how's it going?"

"I'm good, thanks. I am sorry to inconvenience you at this particular time, but I was in need of a hammer, and I wondered if you would have one to lend," Brad said.

Garrett, thrown off by Brad's use of such politeness, paused.

Why is he talking like this?

He had never sounded this way. Their usual conversations, which Garrett would try to avoid as much as possible, usually included "guy talk" with some four-letter words sprinkled in here and there. He had never seen Brad so friendly. It took Garrett a second to gather his thoughts.

"Uhh, yes. Yes, I think I do. Let me open the garage, and I will meet you out there," Garrett said, puzzled.

Brad turned around and took a step off the porch without saying a word.

Garrett opened the door leading to the garage and hit the white button on the wall. He watched as the garage opened, the motor humming like a well-oiled machine.

The slowly opening door revealed the shadow of Brad's legs, then the rest of him. He stood there blankly.

Garrett stepped down. The cold concrete felt good and cool on his bare feet.

"I'm surprised you of all people don't have a hammer, but I think I have two. Let me check over here," Garrett said as he moved his golf bag out of the way. He walked to the wall closest to the McPherson house and reached for the hammer sitting on top of a small, red toolbox on wheels. "Will this one do?" Garrett said and turned to Brad, who was now behind him.

"I think I need one of smaller size," Brad said, looking down at the floor.

"Oh, okay," Garrett said. He turned, looking at Brad, studying him. Brad was paying no attention to him. "Let's see, I think I have one in here," Garrett said, opening the top drawer of his toolbox.

Brad's expression changed as he lurched toward Garrett. Brad was almost on top of him, his hand reaching for Garrett's head. Garrett hit it out of the way with his arm, but Brad barely moved.

"What are you doing?" Garrett said, trying to push Brad off of him, struggling to breathe with the weight on his chest.

Brad, overpowering him, clenched both of Garrett's hands into one of his, reaching for Garrett's head with the other. Garrett was kicking, amazed at the strength and weight of Brad on top of him. Garrett grunted, trying to get away, letting out a couple of "*ugghhs*" trying to break free.

A thought zapped through Garrett, and he realized he needed to push himself up. He had to move quickly, his arms flailing wildly. He was running out of time and options. He had to do it now, or he would lose this fight. Garrett arched his back, gaining just enough leverage to deliver a direct headbutt to Brad's face. Brad let out a shriek that didn't sound human. It was a squeal that traveled through the garage and hurt Garrett's ears. He winced.

Garrett, now able to stand, was face to face with Brad.

"Brad, what are you doing? What is going on?" Garrett said, out of breath.

Brad's face, full of hatred, lurched for Garrett again. Garrett moved out of the way and Brad hit the toolbox, scattering tools all over the floor with a loud boom. Brad turned back and looked at Garrett, this time wearing something that looked like a smile.

"Come on!" Garrett said, now fearing for his life. The adrenaline was pumping through his body, and survival instincts had taken over. For a second, he even thought he saw Brad's eyes turn a weird shade of yellow.

Brad, wiggling his fingers, jumped at Garrett, only this time Garrett was ready. A loud thud cracked in the air as Garrett hit Brad in the head with a hammer. Brad fell to the ground, knocking over Garrett's recycling, sending plastic bottles and pieces of cardboard across the floor. Brad's legs twitched and then went still.

What just happened?

Garrett walked over to Brad's body, the hammer still raised in defense. With a brief hesitation, he reached out his arm to check for a pulse. Brad, on his side, let out a gasp of air as his right arm fell to the floor with a thud. Garrett, out of reaction, jerked his hand back into his side.

Shock was setting in, and Garrett shuddered. He reached out a hand that he couldn't keep steady to check again for a pulse. There wasn't one.

Brad's body, lying on the oil-stained floor, began to change to a dark green color. His open eyes changed to a bright yellow. The thing lying on Garrett's garage floor no longer looked human. Garrett, unsure of what it was he was looking at, stood completely still, frozen with fear.

He walked out of his garage backward and reached into his pockets for his phone. His hands were still shaking. He didn't take his eyes off the thing.

Realizing his phone was still in the pants he took off when he got home, he started toward the door. A voice came from behind him, sending a chill down his spine. Garrett froze.

"Garrett?" It was Brad Bayner.

Garrett turned around, stunned.

"I don't know what happened. What day is it?" Brad asked, looking confused.

"What do you mean?" Garrett asked, the hammer still in his hand. He tightened his grip.

"I…I uh, woke up on my bedroom floor," Brad said and rubbed his eyes like he had just awakened from a nap. He seemed frightened. "Garrett, what day is it?"

Garrett opened his mouth to answer.

There was a sound of a door closing to their right. The Kleins walked out onto their porch, Mr. Klein helping Mrs. Klein down the steps. They walked toward Garrett and Brad holding hands, Garrett glancing at Brad and then back to the Klein's. He studied all of them carefully like they were all complete strangers.

"We don't really know what happened," Mr. Klein said. "We woke up in our bed, and I just checked my cell phone, and it must be off. Either my phone has gone crazy, or we slept for a couple of days," he said with a slight chuckle. "What is today?" Mr. Klein asked. Mrs. Klein smiled but had a scared look on her face. "We don't really remember going to bed or waking up, but here we are. Here we are three or four days later."

Something had just been uncovered, but no one realized it. Garrett had killed a *Being*. In doing so, he released every victim that creature had ever taken over. In this case, Brad Bayner and the Kleins. Like being in a coma, they didn't know how long they had been out.

"I don't know what's going on, but I think we need to call the police. There is something in my garage I want to show you guys. You won't believe what just happened to me," Garrett said. He was still shaking. He led them up his driveway and into the garage. The thing lay there, yellow, blank eyes staring into nothing. It reeked.

Garrett pointed at it with his free hand. "This thing attacked me. But here is the craziest part- when it came to my door, it looked just like you, Brad. It pretended to... be you," Garrett said, not realizing he was still holding his hammer. Mrs. Klein buried her face in Mr. Klein's shoulder.

"Like me?" Brad said, looking down at the thing.

"Yes, like you. I can't explain it. It tried to kill me. So I...I killed it with this hammer," Garrett said, somehow feeling a touch of guilt.

"We need to call the police. I'm scared," Mrs. Klein said.

"I was just on my way to do that. I will grab my phone. You guys can follow me inside, so you don't have to stand out here with this thing," Garrett said to the group.

They walked single file, confused, keeping as far away from the creature as they could. They all, except for Mrs. Klein, stared at it as they passed.

They made their way into Garrett's kitchen as he walked to his bedroom to grab his phone. He came back to them, now calming down.

"You guys can have a seat. I think we are all in for a long night. Does anyone want anything to drink?" Garrett asked. Mr. Klein was using Garrett's counter as a handrail, like someone roller skating for the first time, too scared to let go of the side rail. They all sat at the kitchen table, and he gave them each a bottle of water.

Garrett tapped on his phone to dial 911 for the third time in three days. He desperately wanted to check on his parents. He was thinking about Laura. Everything was happening around him so fast. He closed his eyes and wished he could be anywhere else.

- 142 -

CHAPTER 28

It took a half-hour for a police officer to arrive. The officer pulled into Garrett's driveway, a muffled voice going off on his radio. He walked up to Garrett's door and knocked lightly. He took a few steps back, looking at Garrett's landscaping.

Next door, the McPhersons, who had not been saved, still lay where they had since Saturday.

A creature wearing the face of Chad McPherson was pacing around the McPherson living room. It had watched the whole thing happen from the window. When the thing saw Brad Bayner and the Klein's talking with Garrett in the middle of the street, it knew what had happened. It felt no sympathy for what it had done to the McPherson family. It would have gladly killed them if it came to that, but they went with little effort. But these things did feel sympathy for their own, and this one was feeling a deep sorrow now.

These *Beings* were clever, but their range of emotion was limited. The more people they overtook, the more they were able to feel. Sadness was not an emotion they felt before entering this world, but they were slowly learning and evolving. As this one, still in the form of Chad, paced up and down the hall of the McPherson home, it felt a new emotion start in its belly and slog its way up to its brain; *revenge.*

Garrett was holding a water bottle up to his lips when he heard a knock at the door. The Klein's and Brad looked at the door as if they had just heard a gunshot. Garrett looked around at everyone with a comforting glance.

"I'll go with you," Brad said, still seeming sluggish. He followed Garrett to the door, standing behind him the whole time.

Garrett looked out the top of the door and saw the officer standing on his porch. He opened the door with relief.

"Garrett Bradley?" The officer said, sounding accusatory.

"Yes, I am Garrett," Garrett said as he walked out onto the porch. Brad followed closely behind.

"Garrett, I'm officer Anthony Delgada with the Burnley Police Department. I'm here about a disturbance call," the officer said in a no-nonsense tone. Even though he was younger, he reminded Garrett of one of those smart but serious detectives from the old 60s TV shows.

"Yeah, this is going to sound crazy, I know, so I will have to show you in the garage," Garrett said, passing the officer, heading toward his garage, and making a motion to follow him.

Garrett led. The officer let Brad go ahead and then followed them both.

"So, what is the issue here? What can I do for you?" Delgada said, having no time for small talk. He acted inconvenienced.

"This is going to sound crazy," Garrett said, rubbing his neck. "But this thing attacked me. It tried to kill me in my garage. When it came to my door, it looked just like Brad," he said, pointing to Brad. Delgada looked Brad up and down. "I killed him out of self-defense. It was going to kill me."

Delgada spit saliva mixed with chewing tobacco. A brown splatter hit Garrett's driveway. "I've seen a lot of crap in my day, but this takes the cake. I'm waiting for the damn camera man to come out and tell me I'm on a TV show," Delgada said and wet his lips. Garrett didn't know if he believed him or not, but the way he was looking at him, he was sure he didn't.

Garrett, ignoring that comment, continued. "And then after I killed it, Brad and Mr. and Mrs. Klein came out their front doors, almost at the same time, and told me they didn't remember going to bed, and they didn't know what day it was."

The Klein's came around the corner as Garrett was saying this. Mrs. Klein still had her head buried in her husband's shoulder.

Delgada looked at all of them and laughed. "I don't know what you guys have been smoking, but it sure does seem like the good stuff." He snorted. "Good God, this one takes the cake," his growing grin showed his disbelief.

"I know this seems crazy, but it's true. I woke up and had no idea what day it was. They had the same thing happen to them," Brad said, pointing to the Klein's.

Mr. Klein nodded. Mrs. Klein didn't look up.

Delgada paused. "Alright. Well…I'll humor you all. Has anyone checked on your neighbors in that house?" He pointed at the McPherson home.

Garrett's heart dropped. The pit came back to his stomach and worked its way up to his throat. He felt sick thinking about something happening to the McPherson children. He pictured the cat again.

I'm so sorry, Snowy.

"No. No, we haven't," Garrett's voice croaked.

Delgada looked at them all and grinned. "Well then, I'll go take a look," he said and spit again.

He walked over to the McPherson house, shaking his head. He walked through their side yard, stepping over a red plastic baseball bat that was snuggled next to a blue bike turned on its side. Delgada stepped up on to their porch and noticed the yellow and pink chalk that covered the sidewalk in a perfect five-year-old graffiti handwriting.

He rang the doorbell and took a step back. He looked up at the sun, whistled a few beats of an old country song, and spit in the grass.

The door opened, and Chad McPherson peeked his head out nervously.

"Hello, officer. Is there anything in that which I can help?" Chad said, his English sounding like a foreign exchange student taking lessons.

"Maybe you can," Delgada said and smiled a conceited smile. He pointed to Garrett, Brad, and the Kleins. "Your neighbors over there had a little scare tonight, so I am just doing a welfare check. Everyone here doin' ok? Have you guys heard anything or noticed anything out of the ordinary?"

"Oh, dear. There has not been anything which I have seen nor heard," Chad said. He seemed peculiar. He was still halfway behind the door as if he were hiding something.

"Is anyone else here? Would you mind if I came in to take a look?" Delgada said, trying to peer inside.

"Oh, I am afraid that will not be a necessary task. No one is home but I. The children are home, of course, but they are sleeping," Chad said with a forced smile.

"Well, maybe we should wake them up, I'll just ask them a question or two, and then I will be on my way," Delgada said, making direct eye contact with Chad.

"No, no, no. That won't be necessary," Chad said and began to shut the door.

Delgada stopped the door with his hand. Chad looked up at him with uncomfortable eyes. Delgada put his hand on the radio next to his shoulder. He didn't get a word out before Chad grabbed him by the throat. Chad lifted Delgada with ease, Delgada struggling to grab his gun. Chad, who had now partially formed into a *Being*, showing its yellow eyes and teeth, slammed him against the vinyl siding next to the front door.

Brad and Garrett rushed to help Delgada. The thing was squeezing Delgada's throat so hard he felt a pop in his left eye. His vision went cloudy, and he tried to turn to see what was happening out of his right eye. He closed his eyes, hoping it would clear his vision, but it only seemed to make it worse. He could feel warmth on his cheek as blood slowly dripped out of his left eye, flowing like a tear. More blood oozed out as Garrett and Brad came running up screaming.

Delgada tried to talk but couldn't. He was gargling, and the darkness from his left eye made its way over to the right. He was now completely blind. He tried to scream but was gargling his own saliva and blood. He pointed to his gun with a shaky finger.

Garrett yelled to the Kleins, "Call the police, hurry!" They walked as fast as they could to their home.

Garrett reached for the thing's hands, trying to free Delgada, Brad simultaneously reaching for Delgada's gun. The creature let out a sound that sounded like a hiss and showed its long tongue. A faint smile was on its face, seeming to enjoy the altercation. Garrett noticed the mildew smell again.

Brad was able to get one hand on Delgada's gun and lifted on the handle. Delgada was kicking, being whipped around like a child carrying a doll by its hair. The gun, now almost secure, flew to the grass as Brad's hand fell to his side. The thing, now holding Delgada with its left hand, had put the four-inch blade of its right index finger through Brad's skull. He fell to the ground.

Garrett turned and grabbed the gun, adrenaline making his hands shake. He paused, unsure if he could shoot the thing that looked like his neighbor. Guilt and hesitation flowed in his head. His palms were sweaty. He had to do it. He lifted it, aimed, and pulled the trigger.

Dark green and black liquid went everywhere. Garrett had shot the thing directly between the eyes. Its head splattered all over the vinyl siding. The door and the porch were covered in it. It fell and Delgada toppled over beside it. They were both dead. The smell seemed worse now.

Just like what happened in Garrett's garage, the thing slowly formed back into a dark green mess. Garrett ran inside just as the McPherson family was waking.

Now he understood.

CHAPTER 29

"What happened?" Alyssa McPherson asked.

"If I told you, I don't know that you'd believe me," Garrett said, out of breath. He was relieved to see everyone alive, the children squinting their eyes in the bright light they hadn't seen for days.

The McPherson family was standing in their living room now.

"What's going on? Why are you here?" Chad McPherson asked, puzzled.

"I will explain later. The police are on their way," Garrett said. Chad and Alyssa frowned, both opening their mouths to speak.

"Everyone in your family is safe. Everyone is okay. That's all you need to know for now. The police will be here any minute. I'm sorry, but I have to get to my parents."

He motioned for Chad to join him in the kitchen. He heard one of the kids ask for a snack.

"Don't let anyone look outside. It's a mess. I will explain later. For now, stay inside and stay together. Trust me."

Chad looked confused, not yet alert enough to think clearly. Nothing was registering with him, and his eyes held a perplexed blankness.

Garrett ran out the door. The Kleins were standing in the middle of the street, Mrs. Klein talking on a cell phone.

"They're alright," Garrett said. Mr. Klein's expression changed from worried to relieved.

"Thank God," Mr. Klein said.

"I think you guys should go inside and lock the door. Stay together. The police will be here any minute. I have to go check on my parents. Are you good?"

Mr. Klein hesitated. "Yes, we're fine, Garrett. Go check on your parents. We will be just fine here."

Garrett nodded. He felt responsible for them as if they were his own parents. He turned, ran to his house, opened the door, and grabbed his keys. The adrenaline was working overtime in Garrett's body now. He locked the door, hopped in his car, and took off. Two police cars turned into the neighborhood as he exited. He relaxed in his seat.

Garrett thought he understood now, but he couldn't come to terms with it. He played everything out in his head, trying to make sense of the events of the last hour and a half. He understood some sort of creature was taking on the form of humans. He didn't know how or why.

How is this possible?

He wasn't aware that these creatures were adapting to their new habitat. He didn't understand they were learning how humans interacted, what they ate, what they said, what they watched on TV, or how they treated each other. They were evolving, and they were trying to stay one step ahead of humans.

Oh, they already were one step ahead.

After an eternity of weaving in and out of traffic, Garrett arrived at his parents' house, thankful he hadn't been pulled over for speeding. He ran up to the doorstep and tried the door. It was locked. He knocked on it, ringing the doorbell simultaneously. The anticipation made him want to scream.

His dad answered the door.

"Hey, pops. Is mom here, too? Are you guys alright?" he said, running inside, passing his father.

Something isn't right here.

"Garrett, everything is fine. Why on Earth do you speak this way?"

When the words left his lips, Garrett knew. There was no "*Hey, boy.*" It was English that sounded much too proper for Jerry Bradley. Garrett knew what he had to do, hoping he could do it.

Garrett stared at it. He faked one way, then ran upstairs as fast as he could. The thing, realizing what Garrett was doing, chased after him, still looking like Jerry Bradley. Garrett got upstairs first and entered their bedroom. He saw both of their bodies in their bed.

"Mom! Dad!" Garrett yelled. His voice screeched with panic. They didn't move.

The thing entered the bedroom, its yellow eyes fixated on Garrett. It jumped for him, extending the blade on its finger. Garrett jumped out of the way, and the creature's claw went through the wall and stuck there.

This is it. Kill it or be killed.

Garrett came prepared.

The *Being* was hissing as it tried to free its hand, stuck deep inside the drywall. Crumbled pieces fell and flew in every direction. Garrett knew what he had to do. This time, *he* was one step ahead.

He pulled Delgada's gun out from the back of his pants and fired. It fell to the ground. Black and green plastered on the wall and floor. The smell filled the bedroom.

Garrett turned and looked at his parents. He knew what to expect now.

They were alive.

"Garrett? What are you doing here?" his mom asked, raising herself up from her side of the bed.

He pulled out his phone to call Laura.

CHAPTER 30

"Hello?" Laura said from the other end of the phone. Her voice was comforting to Garrett.

"Laura! Where are you? Are you home?" Garrett almost yelled into the phone.

"I just got home from work. Are you okay?" Laura asked, sounding concerned. She stood up from her couch and started pacing.

"Don't leave. Lock your doors. I am coming to get you," Garrett said, his parents watching him from their bed, confused.

"What are-"

"I don't have time to explain," Garrett said, raising his voice.

"I..umm, okay," Laura said. She started pacing faster out of fear.

"I'll be there soon. Lock your doors. Don't answer the door, and don't let anyone in. I'll see you soon." Garrett hung up the phone before she had a chance to respond.

"Garrett, what's going on?" Mrs. Bradley said as she put her feet on the floor and stood up slowly from the bed, struggling a little, the way older folks do. She looked down and gasped at the mess on the floor.

"I'll explain in the car. Trust me. But we've got to go. Now!"

Garrett helped his father up from the bed and gathered some of their clothes.

"Where's your suitcase? You're going to stay with me for a while," he said, still gathering their things. He didn't look up at them as he gathered more clothes in a pile.

Mr. Bradley grabbed Garrett by the arm. "What is it?"

"I'll tell you in the car, we don't have time now," Garrett said, wiping sweat from his forehead.

"I'll grab the suitcase," Jerry said and walked to the closet. He came back a minute later with a green and blue suitcase that looked about twenty years old. He threw it on the bed and unzipped it. Garrett threw the things he had gathered inside, then zipped it closed. The zipper felt new and closed with ease. He led his parents out the door as fast as they would move.

A few miles down the road, Garrett caught his breath and began to think rationally. He felt as if he had been watching himself from a distance. It all felt surreal. He felt like he was a character in a movie that he didn't audition for and had no interest in playing. He didn't know if things would get worse or get better, but he knew one thing for sure; he was going to do everything in his power to keep his parents and Laura safe. Whatever it took.

"Tell us what's going on, honey," Mrs. Bradley said from the back seat.

"This isn't going to make any sense, but I will try. I was attacked by my neighbor, the one that lives across from me. I don't think you guys have ever met him. Anyway, he came to the house, and he asked if he could borrow something, then attacked me in the garage. He didn't just attack me, he tried to kill me." He was starting to get worked up now. "I hit him in the head with a hammer and killed him."

His parents gasped. Jerry looked back at his wife.

"When I killed him, he turned into a green…*thing*. Like a creature. Some sort of *Being*. I called the cops to try to explain everything to them. An officer came out, and he went over to the neighbor's, you know them, the McPherson's. Well, when he got there, Chad McPherson attacked the officer and killed him. I shot him. I killed him, too. I mean, I killed *it*, too."

Angela Bradley put her hand on Jerry's shoulder. Her eyes were wet with tears. Jerry sat dumbfounded.

"But here's the crazy part. The part that has sent ice-cold chills through me. When these things died and turned into that green glob of mess, the people they looked like came back, like they had been sleeping right through everything! It happened to you guys, too. The thing in your bedroom, I killed it, and then I watched you guys wake up. You were asleep on your bed like you were taking a nap."

"I don't understand," Jerry said. "Are you saying these things can take on the form of humans? And if so, what are they?"

"Yes, I think they can. And I don't know what they are. Here's what I know; I've come in contact with three of them now. And each one of them had some peculiar way of talking. Almost like they were using old English…or something. I don't know. But it's broken English. Like they are just learning it," Garrett said. In that second, his brain made the connection. He understood these things were starting to evolve. They were learning as they went along. They had everything figured out except the language.

But they were getting there.

Garrett's mind drifted, taking it all in. His car drifted with his mind. A car honked at him, and he swerved back into his lane. His apology was a friendly wave.

"So what are we going to do, Garrett?" Jerry said. "You need to call the police again. Let them handle this."

"I saw what happened when I tried that. We need to do more than that. The problem is going to get people to believe it." He was speeding now. His parents gave each other a hopeful glance. "We need to get a message to the news or social media or…something. We have to let everyone know what's going on. That's really our only chance of saving people."

"And do what?" Mrs. Bradley yelled. Jerry could sense the undertone of anger and fear in her voice. She sat upright, almost between Garrett and Jerry, leaning over from the back seat. "You're going to go on the news and tell everyone that aliens are coming, and they are taking over? You'll end up in jail or the looney bin, one of the two," she said and slid back into her seat. A look of defeat crept across her face.

"It's ok, dear. I am sure we will get through this. Whatever *this* is," Jerry said. He half-turned and smiled at her. "Where are we going, Garrett?"

Garrett straightened his face. "We have to go get Laura."

CHAPTER 31

The Bradleys, all three of them, pulled up to Laura's condo. Garrett hopped out, looking around in a matter of self-defense, then helped his parents out of the car and up to Laura's door. He knocked, then stepped back, feeling the gun pressed against his lower back.

Laura answered the door with a look of panic on her face.

"Laura, are you alright?" Garrett asked. He had one hand behind him on the handle of the gun. His parents stood behind him and noticed this, and Jerry brought his wife closer to him.

"Yes, I'm fine, Garrett. What's going on? I'm starting to freak out a little here."

Garrett breathed a sigh of relief, hearing Laura sound like herself. There was no English that sounded like it came from an old black and white movie, and it wasn't broken. Laura was Laura.

Thank God.

"Can we come in? We need to talk," Garrett said. He could feel his body starting to regain its control. He was suddenly feeling like himself again, aware and alert. He realized he needed a drink of water badly. For the first time in a few hours, his face was showing color, and his green eyes returned to their normal, calm state.

Laura led them to her living room. Garrett noticed the same fragrance he smelled the night of their first date. This made him forget about everything that was happening around him for a few seconds.

"Laura, this is my mom and dad. Angela and Jerry," he said, waving them over.

"It is so nice to meet you," Angela said, grinning from ear to ear. We've heard a lot about you. We weren't sure if Garrett was ever going to find a girlfriend."

Garrett's face displayed a shade of red on his cheeks, but he didn't care.

Laura, meet my parents. Maybe they'll be your in-laws one day. Oh, by the way, the world is ending.

Jerry interrupted quickly. "We are so glad to meet you, Laura. I think what Angela is trying to say is that we have heard only good things about you," he said, trying to let the awkwardness pass.

Laura looked at Garrett and smiled.

"Well, your son is very sweet. I like having him around," Laura said and took Garrett's hand. He looked at his parents and smiled. They offered a smile back.

Laura grabbed a blanket from the couch, folded it, and threw it on the back of a chair in the corner. "Please, sit," she said and gestured to the couch. "Would you like anything to drink?"

"Water would be fine, please," Angela said as she sat, holding Jerry's hand.

"Of course. I'll go grab some," Laura said, turning toward the kitchen.

"I'll give you a hand," Garrett said and followed her.

They entered the kitchen, and Laura's smile turned into a look of bewilderment.

"What's going on, Garrett?" she said. Garrett could see she was getting upset.

He grabbed her by the hips and pulled her toward him. It started with a small kiss but quickly escalated into a kiss fueled by passion. Garrett's hands instinctively went for her shirt, but he stopped himself. He realized, now more than ever, just how much he cared for her. He backed away from her, her eyes closed, still hanging on to the kiss.

"This is going to sound crazy, but please, hear me out. Since I have been home from work, I've seen two… *things* murdered. One tried to kill me, and the other one killed my neighbor and a police officer. They.." he paused, noticing how insane he must have sounded to her.

He took a breath and continued. "When these things were killed, they transformed into some sort of green creature."

She looked at him and frowned.

"I know. I know it sounds crazy, but trust me! These things are out there, and they are somehow taking people over. The one that attacked me looked just like my neighbor. When I killed it, it transformed, and then my neighbor came out of the house and said he didn't know what day it was."

Laura turned to look out the window, still frowning.

"I wish I could have some cameras come in here and tell you I was pranking you, but it's all true. I swear," Garrett said, pleading his case. He was exhausted and had a headache.

Laura raised her head, and her eyes widened.

Social media post.

"I saw a post online. They were saying there was safety and shelter at the old LBD building downtown. One comment said they had food, shelter, and medicine. I wonder if it has anything to do with this? Maybe someone else has seen them too, and now a group of people are hiding in there to stay safe. I thought they were crazy or something, but maybe that's what this is all about."

"Maybe we should check it out. Maybe it'll help us get to the bottom of what's really going on. I had my parents pack a few things, but I was just going to have them stay with me for a while. What about your family? Maybe you should call them," Garrett said, sounding concerned.

"Well, they are a state away. If this is real, I wonder if this is happening everywhere? My mind is still in shock trying to process this," she said, pouring a glass of water for Mrs. Bradley.

"Here, let me take this to my mom. You call your family and check on them," Garrett said, grabbing the water. He kissed her again, and they both smiled. She pulled her phone out of her back pocket and held it up to her ear.

Garrett walked into the living room and handed his mother the glass of water. "She's calling her parents to check on them," Garrett said and sat down in the chair in the corner.

"Do they live close by?" Jerry said.

"No, they are in Cleveland. Hopefully, nothing like this is happening over there," Garrett said, trying to sound optimistic.

The TV was on the local news channel, and a breaking news alert came on the bottom of the screen. The words scrolled across the bottom and stated, "The Governor to hold a press conference at 4:30 pm EST."

Laura came back into the room and stared at the TV. She was worried now. "They didn't answer. I will try to call them back in a little while."

She sat down on a chair on the other side of Garrett. She noticed what was happening on the TV and grabbed the remote to turn up the volume. As she did so, the governor walked up to the podium.

"My fellow Michiganders, today we have learned of a horrific tragedy in our great state. I am being told by the CDC and Alcob Corp that a deadly viral infection is sweeping the Midwest at an alarming rate. This virus, which seems to make

people hallucinate, has been detected in nine counties. Local government..."

Garrett stood up and yelled at the TV. "This is no virus. They are covering their asses. They need to tell us what's really going on. We are being invaded. They just don't want to say it."

"...At this time, we are implementing a statewide quarantine for fourteen days, similar to that of COVID-19 protocols. We are asking that people not leave their houses, except for emergencies, or to seek shelter at local safe haven shelters provided by the government around the state. My staff and I are meeting around the clock to ensure that everyone in the state of Michigan is safe, and we feel these are the necessary steps to take at this time."

Laura looked at Garrett when the governor mentioned the safe haven. Her phone rang. She stood up. "Hello?" she said as she walked into the kitchen.

"Something is going on here," Garrett said. "Something bigger than we know."

"Maybe they don't even know, yet" Jerry said, looking at the TV.

They continued to watch the press conference in silence, listening to the media ask question after question, none of them getting answered fully. Garrett felt like this was intentional.

Do they know something? What are they hiding?

Laura walked back into the room, this time looking relieved. She made her way over to the chair and sat. "My parents are fine. Everyone is safe. In fact, my brother was just there visiting." She sighed. "I feel so much better now." She paused and looked up at the ceiling. "Whatever is happening, maybe it's only happening here. The governor did say this was only detected in nine counties."

But it wasn't just happening there. It was happening everywhere. Her parents had just been lucky that it hadn't happened to them yet. It had happened to Jeff and Sarah Nielsen in their little cabin on the lake. It happened to Dave Langley. It was happening in Seattle, New York, Los Angeles, and Miami. There was no safe place. There was nowhere to run. It was all closing in on them, and there was nowhere to hide.

CHAPTER 32

Garrett and Laura's phones chimed in unison with an email from their employer. Garrett pulled out his phone and checked it.

"Due to unforeseen circumstances, BelTech will remain closed until Monday, August 15th. Any employee who needs to come to the office to grab any belongings can do so tomorrow, from 8am–10am. Please grab all necessary materials to be able to work remotely until that time. Please email your supervisor for any additional information. Thank you, Bill MacMillan, CEO."

"Well, I guess we are on lockdown now," Garrett said, locking his phone and placing it back in his pocket. He stood up, looked out the window, and rubbed his eyes. "This is nuts. I feel like I'm watching a movie or something."

Was the pandemic the start of all of this? I need some answers.

"It'll be alright, Garrett. The government will figure this out soon, and then we will go on like normal," Jerry said and placed his hand on his wife's leg.

Garrett nodded and raised his eyebrows. Inside, he didn't believe it at all. He looked over at Laura. "Laura found a post on social media. Maybe we could go down there until this thing blows over. It's one of these safe havens the governor is talking about. There are a lot of people who have gone down there seeking shelter. Maybe we'll be safer if we are around a bigger group. People will be less likely to be…" He struggled for the right word. "Taken over," Garrett said, looking at his parents.

Jerry said, "If you think it's the right thing to do, then we should do it. What do you say, hon?"

Angela nodded. "I want to stay with you, whatever we do. If you think that's best, then let's do it. We could always go down and see what it's like, and if we don't want to stay, it's not like they can force us."

Garrett nodded and looked at Laura. "What do you think?"

"I'm scared. I don't want to be alone. I want to be with you all," she said, smiling at Garrett's parents. They smiled back at her. "I will pack a few things."

"Okay. Okay, good. We need to stop back by my house and grab a few things, too," Garrett said. He had worry written on his face, but was feeling better about their decision.

Laura pulled out her phone and checked the post again. "This post has exploded. The last time I checked it, it said there were about five hundred people there. Now there's over two thousand."

"Then we should go sooner than later. They might start turning people away," Garrett said as he stood. "Grab what you need for a few days. Don't forget a phone charger." He suddenly felt like a dad double-checking what his children were bringing on a long road trip. He had helped his parents pack their bags earlier, and the irony was not lost on him.

Laura got up and disappeared behind the door of her bedroom. Garrett looked at his parents, trying to read them. He studied them for a moment. He didn't know what was going to happen to them. He didn't know about anything anymore. Whatever happened, right now in this moment, he was grateful for his parents. They gave him the best life he could ever have asked for. He realized how fast life had gone for him. He remembered playing basketball, looking up at his dad, his dad beaming with pride. His dad cheering him on with his jet-black hair. That jet-black hair had turned gray now, and it made him sick to his stomach for a minute how little he appreciated everything his parents had given him in his life. He sat there, taking it in, savoring the mental picture he had made in his mind. He told himself he would keep the picture of them sitting on Laura's couch etched in his brain forever. But it never works that way. The picture always ends up fading away.

Everything fades away.

Laura returned with a small bag from her bedroom. Garrett stood up, helped his parents off the couch, then offered to take her bag. She accepted and handed it to him.

"Have everything you need for a few nights?" He asked Laura.

"Yes." She bit at her cheek in deep thought. "Should be good to go."

"I don't anticipate us being there long. Just enough to get through these next few days until things have calmed down," he said, but he didn't know if he believed it. Angela was happy to hear that.

Jerry grabbed Angela's hand as Garrett flung Laura's bag over his shoulder.

"Ok. Let's roll," Garrett said.

Laura opened her front door, and the four of them walked out, unsure of what was waiting for them.

Chapter 33

They made the drive over to Garrett's, forming a game plan on how they wanted to handle the next few days.

The plan was simple; stay together. If anyone went to the restroom, they were to take someone with them. Under no circumstances would anyone be alone at any time. It was as simple as that.

When they pulled up to Garrett's house, there was a firetruck, two police cars, and two ambulances. The coroner had been gone for about thirty minutes.

The McPhersons were outside chatting with the police, giving them the rundown from their perspective on what had transpired. Brad Bayner and officer Delgada's bodies had been placed in the back of the white van and hauled off like two slabs of meat someone had ordered from a butcher.

One of the ambulances was over at the Klein residence. The lights still flashed, but the vehicle was silent. Garrett hopped out of the car and ran over to their house.

Mrs. Klein was on a stretcher with a cool, wet cloth placed on her forehead. Mr. Klein stood beside her, holding her hand. He looked up and saw Garrett.

"What happened?" Garrett said, first looking at Mr. Klein, then looking down at her.

"They want to take her for observation," Mr. Klein said, now putting both of his hands around her hand. "She was complaining of chest pain. I think from all the commotion."

Garrett reached out and touched her shoulder.

"You're going to be just fine. Let them take care of you. Get some rest, and this whole thing will blow over," Garrett said, a sincere look coming from his eyes. They reminded him of his grandparents, both taken by cancer in the last four years.

Mrs. Klein smiled at Garrett.

The stretcher, yellow and black, raised in the air and was placed in the ambulance by two technicians. It jerked and clicked, then rolled backward with ease.

"I'll be right there, darlin'," Mr. Klein said. He turned toward Garrett. "Garrett, what happened? What are those things?"

"Go be with her," Garrett said, extending his hand. Mr. Klein took it and the two shook hands. "I'll explain later. We are going to be gone for a few days, and I am sure they will keep her overnight. I'll call you soon and check on both of you. Don't worry. All of it will be over soon."

With that, Garrett turned back toward his house, where his parents and Laura were waiting for him in the driveway.

"Is everything okay?" Jerry Bradley asked.

"They are taking Mrs. Klein in for observation. She saw everything that had happened earlier, and I'm sure she's just traumatized. They'll probably keep her overnight," Garrett said as he reached into his pocket for his keys.

The four of them stood there as Garrett unlocked the door. He opened it and let the three of them enter before him. He shut it, then locked it from the inside.

"You guys have a seat. I won't be long. I'm going to grab what I need to get me by for a few days until we can come back here and figure the rest of whatever this is out." Garrett told them.

None of them sat.

"Garrett, I'm scared," his mother said.

Garrett noticed a slight tremble in her hands. Her face was white, stricken with fear and grief. For the first time, he thought, he saw his parents in a new light. He was as old as his father was when he bounced Garrett on his knee. Garrett felt a responsibility toward his parents to take care of them now. To keep them safe. The Bradley story had shifted, and the realization was that his parents were at that age where the sunset of their life would be here way too soon. A tidal wave of nausea whirlpooled in Garrett's stomach. The whites of his eyes had turned a shade of pink. A tear started to cascade down his cheek. He ran to the bathroom in his bedroom and tried to shut the door with so much force it didn't close. He vomited.

Laura followed, then knocked on the bathroom door.

"Garrett? Are you okay?"

"I'm fine," he said, turning on the cold water in the sink and splashing it on his face. He did this a few times, then rinsed out his mouth.

Laura opened the partially closed door. She put a hand on his shoulder.

The day's events had finally caught up to him. The shock was now almost gone, and it had let reality make its way in. For the first time in a long time, he didn't know what to do.

She hugged him, and he cried into her shoulder.

After a moment, he pulled back.

"Thanks. I guess I needed someone to lean on for a minute."

"You can have me longer than that," she said, smiling.

He went to kiss her, and she put her hand up to stop him.

"Didn't you just puke?" she said, not trying to hold back a laugh.

He laughed. "Yes. Yes, I did."

He bent down, opening the cabinet under the sink. He grabbed a bottle of mouthwash and twisted the cap off, placing it on the sink. He took a gulp, swishing it around in his mouth, throwing his head back to gargle. He spit it out in the sink and turned on the water. They kissed.

In the living room, Jerry Bradley had turned on the TV and sat down with his wife on Garrett's couch. He clicked through a few channels and stopped on the local news. He turned up the volume.

"Authorities are urging anyone who is alone or frightened to come to the LBD building downtown for safety. Local restaurants have pledged to cater food, there are restroom facilities with functioning showers, and St. Matthews Hospital is providing first aid stations. Police are saying this will be set up at least until the quarantine is over. A hotline has been set up for questions anyone may have. Police are also—"

"Garrett? Can you come here, please?" Mr. Bradley said.

Garrett had a flashback of his teenage days; his dad calling him downstairs to reprimand him for not doing a chore or something like that. Something that was almost never worth coming downstairs for in the first place.

Garrett and Laura entered the living room.

"What is it?" Garrett asked.

"They showed the inside of the old LBD factory. They've turned it into a makeshift aid station. They've got people donating food and medicine. I think we are making the right call going," Mr. Bradley said. He looked at his wife, who didn't seem so sure.

"They tell everyone there is a virus going around but then urge people to gather in a group at an old factory that is now a makeshift safe haven. That should tell you it's no virus," Garrett said, staring at the TV.

"Garrett, I don't like it. I don't like it at all," Angela Bradley said. She grabbed the remote and turned off the TV.

CHAPTER 34

"Mom, this is for the best. We will be able to stay with a large group of people, where everyone will be on alert. We need to find more people who really know what's going on so we can figure out how to handle this," Garrett said. He was now sitting next to his parents on the couch.

"I'm just scared. I don't want anything to happen to my boys," Mrs. Bradley said, one hand holding Garrett's hand, the other on her husband's knee.

"I won't let that happen. I won't let anything happen to anyone in this room. I mean it," Garrett said, only now he was looking at Laura. Their eyes met momentarily. She saw a storm brewing behind his eyes.

Garrett stood, now feeling more confident that the decision to go downtown for safety was the right one. He knew he could take care of his three while being able to get to the bottom of whatever this was that was happening.

Inside, he felt like he was playing the lead role in an action movie. The thought made him smile before reality quickly set in, and the fear overtook him again. He shuddered, then looked around to see if anyone had noticed. They hadn't.

"I'm going to finish grabbing my things," Garrett said, then darted down the hall.

He grabbed a few shirts and made sure to get something warm, in case it was cold in the old building. He grabbed a few pairs of socks, underwear, shorts, and one pair of jeans. He placed them all neatly on his bed, then grabbed a small backpack from his closet. He stuffed the clothes in the bag, then zipped it shut.

He walked to his bedroom door and checked out into the hallway to see if anyone was coming. With emotions running wild and the uncertainty lingering in the air, Garrett didn't want anyone to see what he was doing next. He could hear Laura and his father discussing something and acted quickly. He pushed his bedroom door partially closed.

Inside the closet, he grabbed a 9mm gun he had purchased two years ago and had only fired once on the range. He stared at it for a minute, turning it over in his hands. It was black and silver and still felt new. The box of ammo that had sat on the top shelf in his closet for almost two years had never been opened. He grabbed both and walked over to the backpack sitting on the bed.

He opened the box, which felt like cardboard, struggling to do so quietly. A few bullets fell to the floor, and the light bounced off the gold casing as they landed on the carpet. They sounded heavy. Garrett grabbed the two on the floor, then a handful more from the box, and threw them in the side pocket of the backpack. He grabbed a green shirt from his closet, unfolded it, and wrapped the gun in it, carefully. He picked it up, then sat it back down and turned to see if anyone was standing there watching. He unfolded it, checked the safety, then quickly folded it back up. He placed it in the front pocket of the bag, then zipped it closed.

He walked back into his closet and placed the box of ammo on the top shelf of the wire rack, then flicked off the light. His parents in the living room and he in his bedroom hiding what he was doing made him feel like the time he was fourteen, and his friend had given him a dirty magazine he had kept hidden for a week until his mom found it sticking out of his mattress. The memory made him smile and shake his head.

Garrett walked back into the living room with the backpack slung over his shoulder, full and heavy.

"I still think this is the right thing. You guys sure you're okay with this?" Garrett said, switching the backpack to his other shoulder.

"We're with you," Jerry Bradley said, holding his wife's hand.

Angela nodded hesitantly, then spoke. "Garrett, we talked while you were packing. We think this is the right thing to do. Until we get some answers, we think it's best to stay with a large group. We have a better chance of keeping safe there than staying here. We are with you, honey."

Garrett smiled and looked over at Laura, who was also wearing a smile on her face. She nodded in agreement.

"Good. Then let's do this," Garrett said, checking his pockets for his keys, wallet, and phone.

*　　*　　*

At the LBD building, they were setting up more and more cots, herds of people coming in by the hour, searching for safety. Most of the patrons were elderly, some were single mothers with children, and some were families of four and five, hoping they could ride this out here with groups of people who were just as afraid as they were.

The governor had deployed the National Guard, who helped with the setup of individual rooms, aid stations, and food areas where people could eat in groups.

Local restaurants had offered to cater food, while others shut down completely. The state was in complete chaos. Some families stayed at home, worried about a virus that didn't exist. Some people were eager to come to the LBD building, others finding other safe havens setup throughout the state with the help of social media posts like the one Laura had seen.

Social media was inundated with conspiracy theories, claiming the end of the world; one had even claimed that this was a government-induced virus spread to control the minds of all US citizens. Riots had started in the streets, causing the police and National Guard to be on high alert, forming protective perimeters in certain areas of the city.

All of this was playing directly into the hands of these creatures. Humans were turning on humans. It was sad, really, how fast the human race had turned on itself. And in the chaos, under the beautiful summer sky of blue, *Beings* were *everywhere*.

CHAPTER 35

For the second time, Sandy Pickrell had seen them moving about in the courtyard of her apartment complex. Clutching a Bible in her hand, she stared out the window, shaking with fear.

She remembered reading about the end of time in the Bible, knowing God was going to return to Earth like a thief in the night. The thought excited her.

The end of time is near, she thought to herself, as the *Being* she was watching returned to the small pond to the east of the parking lot.

She sat down on the couch, a cloud of dust spreading in the air as the cushion wooshed, letting out air. She put the Bible down on the coffee table and prayed silently.

"Lord, tonight, I will do your will. I am your sword. Use me for your good, to further your kingdom, and drive out the evil. You are my strength, and my prayer is for you to fill me with your holiness to drive out this evil. I will take on this fight, Lord. I will be your hand. Let me use you as a shield. It is my responsibility to end this tonight. Through your righteousness, we will send these demons back to hell where they belong. Where they will suffer. I am yours, Lord. Amen."

She got up and grabbed the Bible sitting on the coffee table. Her cats were purring, rubbing against her legs as she went into the kitchen and poured out two cans of wet food into their bowls. They meowed, running to the clear plastic bowls. They ate, and their lips smacked with each bite. Sandy smiled.

Sandy walked into her bedroom and opened the closet. The sliding doors creaked and wobbled, opening awkwardly, barely hanging on to the tracks they slid in. She pulled the long string, and a light turned on up above her head. She opened the top drawer on the dresser, moved a few items of clothing, then pulled out a revolver she had owned for years. The .38 Special, black with a brown handle, was an Astra 680 she had purchased in 1983. The dim light above reflected off the black metal as she turned it over in her hands. She smelled it, then opened it, revealing three bullets in the cylinder. She closed it with a snap. A demonic smile grew across her face. *Doing the Lord's work*, she thought to herself.

She opened the back sliding door of her apartment, holding the gun in her right hand. Sandy started for the pond where she saw the creature submerge earlier. The full moon was big and bright; it painted the wet grass an off-white color in the courtyard by the pond. A car drove by, the headlights making her shield her eyes, and she hid the gun behind her back as it passed by.

I am your sword. You are my shield.

Her heart was racing as she moved closer to the water. The gun was swinging in her right hand with each step she took. Her right foot slipped where the grass ended, and the dirt became swampy mud. She stood on the bank and held the gun out. She looked up to the sky and closed her eyes.

"Evil spirits, it's time for you to return whence you came," she said, her hands now reaching high in the air. She continued, reciting scripture from the Book of Matthew. "When the unclean spirit is gone out of a man, he walketh through dry places, seeking rest, and findeth none. Then he saith, I will return into my house from whence I came out; and when he is come, he findeth it empty, swept, and garnished. Then goeth he, and taketh with himself seven other spirits more wicked than himself, and they enter in and dwell there: and the last state of that man is worse than the first. Even so, shall it be also unto this wicked generation? Lord, use me to do your works!"

A bubble appeared on the surface. Sandy looked down and pointed the revolver at the water. The water was still. Other than the occasional bullfrog croak, the silence was horrendously deafening.

The night is terrifying.

Two green hands reached out of the water and grabbed Sandy around the ankles, pulling her with so much force her neck cracked. The gun went off in the air as she violently jerked forward. It happened so fast that a thought never entered her mind of what was happening. The gun shot was heard by several. A few people looked out their windows.

Her cats continued to eat their food in the dark.

CHAPTER 36

Laura and the Bradley family made their way to Garrett's car. Garrett looked over at the McPherson house, and a chill ran down his spine as he thought about the sound Delgada made as he lost his life. In all the excitement and adrenaline, Garrett hadn't stopped to think about Delgada and Brad Bayner's deaths. He felt like he needed to vomit again.

"Are you okay?" Laura said, placing her hand on his shoulder.

"I'm fine," he said and sighed. "Crazy day is getting to me."

"I know. It'll be over soon. It won't be long," Laura said, then kissed Garrett on his cheek.

"Hey," Garrett said, his face now turning serious and stone cold. "I'm sorry."

Mr. and Mrs. Bradley got in the back seat of Garrett's car.

"Sorry for what?" Laura said, moving her hair out of her face.

"I took too long." He paused momentarily. "I should have asked you out a long time ago. Everything that has happened the last few days has really given me time to think about the fragility of life. It's too short not to take chances. I should have taken a chance on you a long time ago."

Laura grabbed Garrett's hand. "All that matters is now. Just live for now and tomorrow. Whatever has happened before happened." She kissed him on the lips.

Mr. and Mrs. Bradley sat in the back seat, watching their son kiss his new girlfriend. They smiled at each other, then Jerry took Angela's hand and kissed it.

The car door opened, and Jerry Bradley yelled at his son. "Hey, boy. Would you mind turning the car on? It's hotter than blazes in here!" Jerry said, trying to stifle back a laugh.

Angela Bradley smacked her husband on the arm. "Way to ruin the moment, Dr. Love."

Garrett and Laura laughed, then got in the car.

A few miles down the road, heading for the LBD building, Laura pulled out her phone to check the social media post.

"This is taking forever to load," she said and refreshed the app.

"What is?" Garrett said as he exited, trying to merge with traffic on the interstate.

The sun was going down, the horizon now showing an orange and yellow glow over central Michigan. Under different circumstances, Garrett might have pulled his phone out for a picture. No time for that today.

"I'm trying to find the post about the safe haven, but it won't load," Laura said, staring down at her phone. "It's saying network error now."

"That's weird. I've never had any issues with reception here," Garrett said, looking into his side mirror. He sat upright, grabbing his cell phone from his left pocket. "Try mine."

Laura tapped on his phone, then swiped. "Yours is saying the same thing."

"Will you guys check your phone?" Garrett said, looking into his rearview mirror.

Mrs. Bradley pulled the cell phone they shared out of her purse. She handed it to Jerry, knowing he would have more luck than she would. Angela Bradley believed cellphones and the internet were of the devil, and they should only be used to receive or make calls. Texting was another story. That should have been banned from the beginning.

"I don't have service, either," Jerry Bradley said as he pulled reading glasses from his pocket. He placed them on the bridge of his nose and stared at his phone. Angela noticed he was looking down at his phone from over the top of the reading glasses. This made her smile, but she held back the laugh, turning to look out the window instead.

"Well, this is great," Garrett said, showing frustration. "What if something has changed? We're going to drive down there to find out they are now over capacity, and we can't get in! Now we can't check to see where the other ones are, either." His voice was starting to change pitch and grow louder.

"Garrett," Jerry said from the back seat. "It'll be ok. We should be thankful after everything we've been through that we still have each other right now. Please try to relax."

"I'm relaxed," Garrett said. He massaged his temple, then turned down the cool air coming from the vents. "You know what? I'm actually starving right now. Is anyone else hungry?"

"Now we're talking," Jerry said from the back seat, taking his glasses off and putting them back into his pocket.

Garrett laughed. "We could go to Delaney's and get a couple of sandwiches. Maybe we can just get a few to go or something. If they are even open right now." He looked over at Laura. "I'd ask you to check online, but I don't think that's going to do us any good right now."

Laura nodded in agreement.

Garrett took the exit, heading east, and headed for Delaney's. Delaney's had been a sandwich shop that Garrett used to go to on Friday nights when he went to college. Nothing better than throwing down a crispy BLT on toast when you have been playing beer pong with your buddies all night. Garrett thought about that as they drove in silence, wondering how he was able to maintain his GPA in college. He didn't party a lot, but he partied *enough.*

Too much. Yes, it was too much.

Laura put her head against the window, ready to fall asleep. She thought about her parents, hoping they were safe, hoping her brother was with them or was taking them to a safe haven, the way Garrett did with his parents. The reflections of the trees and the cornfield danced off the window and across her face. She closed her eyes and slept.

CHAPTER 37

Laura was gasping for air, her throat being torn apart by green hands, attached to long, green arms, attached to a *Being* with terrifyingly yellow eyes. Garrett was standing beside her in shock, not moving to help her. She reached for him just as his throat was being slashed from a *Being* that had snuck up behind him. The creature looked like it was smiling.

Always smiling.

Mr. and Mrs. Bradley cried as they saw the couple getting torn apart. Blood was spraying and pooling on the ground, a mixture of Laura's and Garrett's, turning the green grass a sickening shade of dark red.

Laura was still alive, but Garrett- almost killed immediately, was flung to the ground like a crash test dummy. Laura tried to scream for him, blood and saliva flying from the hole where her perfectly smooth, tan skin pulled taut over her Adam's apple had once been. She was choking, drowning in her own blood, the metallic taste in her mouth as she reached for Garrett.

Mr. and Mrs. Bradley ran for her but didn't make it. Jerry Bradley was stabbed in the back, and blood flowed from his nose and mouth as he fell to the ground. Angela Bradley was picked up and thrown against a tree, breaking her neck and back simultaneously, resulting in instant death.

Laura was crawling away, the sticky blood causing leaves and grass to cling to her. The *Beings* stood and watched her, seeming to enjoy her agony and suffering. She made it through a line of trees, through a small puddle of water and mud, and into a clearing on the other side.

Her vision, now starting to blur through tears and loss of blood, showed a dimly lit building on the other side of a fence ahead. To the left of a building was a white sign with blue faded letters that read, "LBD Plastics." She tried to scream for help but could only make a gurgling, choking sound. She could feel her heart rate slow. Something stepped into her blurry vision, casting a shadow over her. She saw green, then, barely, the yellow eyes looking down at her. It reached for her. She tried to scream again, her hands clenched into fists with a handful of grass and leaves.

"Hey! Hey! Laura!" Garrett yelled. He was holding her arms.

She stopped flailing and looked at him. She was confused, not understanding how Garrett had survived.

"I said we're here," Garrett said, smiling. "Must have been some dream."

Laura looked out her window and saw Mr. and Mrs. Bradley. They were smiling, looking into her window, standing in some strange parking lot. She started to cry.

"It's okay. Hey. It was just a dream. See? It's just me," Garrett said, looking into her eyes.

She started to smile and let an awkward laugh escape her mouth.

"Let's go grab a sandwich," Garrett said, helping her sit up.

"Okay," she said. She wiped her eyes with the backs of her hands.

CHAPTER 38

"I'm sorry," she said as she got out of the car. Her eyes were red and puffy, but Garrett thought she was just as beautiful as ever.

"Do you want to talk about it?" Garrett said, pulling out his key fob to lock the doors. Mr. and Mrs. Bradley stood beside them, both with comforting expressions on their faces. Laura felt better when she noticed this.

"No, I'm fine. It was just a dream. It was those… *things.*" Her voice cracked with emphasis on "*things.*"

Jerry Bradley, never one that had the best tactics in his life, interrupted.

"Anybody hungry?" he said, either not noticing his timing couldn't have been more awkward or didn't care that it was.

They had pulled into a new restaurant called "*Izzolina's.*" There was a sign, which looked newly placed in the ground with fresh dirt and no grass around its base.

The sign read, "Italian And Hoagies," which Garrett read with amusement, thinking it an odd combination.

Laura smiled, grabbing Garrett's hand, and the group headed for the door. Garrett opened it, then held it open for everyone to enter. It was dimly lit and completely empty, but the aroma of spices was noticeable and overpowering. A man walked to the counter to greet them. His name tag was white with red letters.

"Good evening. We are actually about to close down with this issue we are having. How do you call it? Quarantine?" His accent was thick, producing a much more authentic feel.

"Understandable. Do you have any sandwiches or anything we could take on the road?" Garrett said, then turned around to look at the decor. The irony was not lost on him, as he realized his first and second out-to-eat experiences with Laura were Italian restaurants. It made him smile inside. Under different circumstances, he imagined this would be a fantastic place for a date night.

"We have stromboli. It's sausage, mozzarella, ham, pepperoni and, let me think, I think we have one with pepper jack cheese." The man said, rubbing his hands together. His name tag read "Enzo."

"We'll take four of them. Whatever you have available is fine," Garrett said and pulled out his wallet.

"You don't have to get ours," Jerry said, reaching for his back pocket.

"I know I don't. But I am," Garrett said, smiling at his father.

Laura batted her eyes and placed her head on his shoulder. She thought he smelled good, trying to hide that she was sniffing his shirt.

"Thank you, honey," Angela said. Jerry closed his eyes and smiled.

"You're welcome," Garrett said. He started to give Enzo his card, then brought his hand back closer to his chest. "Oh, does anyone need anything to drink?" Garrett said, turning around to his parents. Laura was still on his shoulder.

"I'll take a water," Laura said, raising her head from his arm.

"Water would be fine," Garrett's parents said almost concurrently.

Enzo tapped a few buttons on the screen, then bent down out of view. He reappeared with four bottles of water in his hands, then placed them down on the counter.

Garrett handed his card to Enzo, who took it with a smile, then swiped. "Do you need a receipt?"

"No. All good, thanks," Garrett said.

The receipt shot out, and Enzo looked up at the clock on the wall. He yelled something to the workers in the back in Italian. A much younger man, who looked to be about sixteen, came from around the corner with a bag. He placed it on the counter and smiled. Garrett grabbed it.

"Have a good night," Enzo said, smiling.

"You, too. Be safe out there." Garrett said as he passed out the water bottles. Enzo held up his hand and waved.

Jerry held the door open for everyone, and the group made their way to a new-looking picnic table outside.

"Do you guys want to eat here really quick before we hit the road?" Garrett asked, pointing to the picnic table.

"Works for me," Jerry said. He was starting to salivate.

Jerry helped Angela sit down, sitting across from Garrett and Laura. Garrett opened the bag, handing out sandwiches like he was a summer camp counselor on lunch duty.

They ate in silence as the dark was swallowing the light, ready to make this another day marked off on the calendar.

We better hurry.

Angela spoke up. " I know we have said this a dozen times, but, whatever happens, we just all have to promise we stay together. I don't care if one of us has to go to the bathroom. We all go together. Whatever this is, it's scary enough that we should all stay together. Please, just promise me."

"We will, mom. I promise. It'll blow over, and we will laugh about it one day," Garrett said, sounding enthusiastic. Angela reached out and grabbed his hand. Laura looked at their hands and then placed hers on his leg. Garrett had never felt more loved than he did in this moment.

The food had been eaten; the take-out bag had been crinkled and thrown in the trash, and trips inside to the restroom had been a success for all. Garrett's black car reversed out of the parking lot and headed to their destination. It was dark now.

Enzo had sent the rest of his employees home. He counted the money in the register, stuffed it in a white envelope, and took some notes on lined paper that sat on a desk in the back behind the kitchen. He grabbed the trash, twisted it around, and threw it over his shoulder, whistling as he walked. He kicked the back door open, his two hands holding the heavy trash bag over his shoulder. The light in the parking lot buzzed as insects flew around it. Enzo heaved the heavy bag into the dumpster, then turned to lock up for the night, unsure how long they would be closed for this time of quarantine. He had a wife and a baby on the way to think about, and he knew this would hurt financially. He frowned, and the worry of not being a good provider entered his mind.

He turned as he heard something running for him, then ran for the back door as fast as he could. The green hand reached out as Enzo slammed the door shut, and it was caught- wedged between the door and the wall. The thing made a horrifying shriek. Then, as quickly as it all happened, it was over. The thing was gone. Enzo locked the back door, then backed away slowly. His feet shuffled shakily as he backed away from the door. He bumped into something. He turned around, and it was there, staring at him. The claw extended and went through Enzo's chest. It raised him in the air, and his black shoes dangled.

These things were still evolving. They now had all the information they needed. Humans were an easier target than they had expected. The time for inhabiting had come. It was time for them to move to their final stage of preparation. It was time to hunt and kill.

CHAPTER 39

You might call them fireflies, but in the Midwest, they are referred to as *lightning bugs*, and tonight, there were thousands of them in the cornfield that separated Walton and Hatterburg Counties. If you sat and stared, you would see them and their glowing rear ends, seeming to blink in perfect rhythm and harmony. This field, owned by "Big Man" Eddleton, used to go on as far as the eye could see. Sprawling out so far, you would think you were looking at the Atlantic Ocean.

In 2016, however, the Eddleton family had sold a majority of the land when "Big Man" died at the age of 93. Originally, there were talks of an outdoor mall going in place where the corn used to grow freely in the summer sun, but after a few failed attempts, it was sold again- this time to a housing developer. Eddleton would roll over in his grave if he saw the three hundred homes that now sit where he used to work in the unforgiving midwestern heat.

The tops of the cornstalks swayed in the breeze. They made a scraping sound as they touched and danced with the wind. If you looked closely, you would see the thousands of glows tonight, and if you looked closer, even, you would see that they weren't all insects. If you listened, paying no attention to the sounds of the insects and the usual late summer symphony of sound, you would hear the sound of footsteps.

Hunting.

And then you would see the corn forcefully being pushed left and right as dark green bodies moved closer. The tops of those heads, so hideous and disgusting, were peeking out from the top of the corn, smelling swampy from years of sitting in all of those bodies of water, waiting to make their moves. And tonight, here they were. All making their way for the three hundred homes on "Big Man" Eddleton's field.

Hunting.

Earth was one of the last places to inhabit. One would think with all the technology Earth had, the humans would have been ready. The pandemic of 2020 showed otherwise, and it would be foolish to think that these *Beings* didn't know that. No, Earth was woefully ill-prepared for a viral attack, just as they were woefully ill-prepared for this.

While humans watched their reality TV, bought their luxury cars, and concerned themselves only with keeping up with the Joneses, these things waited…and waited…. and waited. And now, they were on the move to put the finishing touches on all of it.

CHAPTER 40

Garrett tried the radio on his car, having no luck. He tried every channel, even going through the auto-tune feature, to find a station with a signal. There was nothing. No golden hits, no talk radio. Nothing. The sound of static was the only station playing tonight, and it was playing loud and proud.

Garrett turned the radio off. "I can't get anything to come through tonight," he said, not taking his eyes off of the road. It was completely dark now, his headlights slashing two perfect circles in the dark, lighting up the road in front of them.

"I still don't have any kind of service, either," Laura said, looking down at her phone.

In the backseat, the two eldest Bradleys slept, their bellies full of Italian flavors and spices. Jerry let out the occasional snore, which made both Laura and Garrett laugh every time. They had only left the restaurant fifteen minutes ago.

Laura put her hand on Garrett's leg. He looked over at her and smiled.

Garrett was still in disbelief, more like a state of shock, at everything that had happened in the last few days. Having Laura near him, although new, comforted him and made him feel better. He still felt like the hero. He was keeping his parents safe; he was keeping his girl safe, and he was taking them all to a safe haven. Even though he wasn't one hundred percent comfortable about what this place was, he still felt it was their best option for survival.

He thought about his job, how working remotely would be, and how he needed to go into the office to grab something. His mind had been elsewhere, with good reason, and he remembered there was a folder on his desk his boss had given him for his new project that he wished he would have had the presence of mind to grab.

"I have to get ahold of my parents," Laura said, interrupting the thoughts in his mind. "I'd feel better if I could talk to them tonight."

"I'm sorry. I can imagine that's not easy," Garrett said, looking over at her.

"I'm sure they are fine, but I hate not knowing," she said and trailed off like another thought had cut her off. "How much longer do you think it'll be?"

"I'm going to go through downtown. Not long. Another thirty minutes or so," Garrett said. He looked in the rearview mirror at his parents.

"Maybe I will take a quick nap," Laura said. She adjusted herself in the seat and then leaned on the passenger side window.

Garrett drove on, feeling his foot getting heavy in anticipation of getting to their safe destination. He was eager to talk to people about what was going on, but he was also exhausted and ready for the trip to be over with. He had been ready for this nightmare of a day to end for hours. He wanted to tell people what he knew.

Laura looked out the window, squinting, trying to make things out in the darkness.

The night is terrifying.

Her eyes were getting heavy, and they had started to roll in the back of her head with drowsiness. She could tell they were passing a field, the two-lane highway they were on running parallel with it. She noticed a small hill. Then another. What were they?

Were those logs? Maybe a tree stump? Trees look less like trees and more like living creatures at night.

Her mind was running on empty. Her eyes were still trying to close, but she was fighting it now. She squinted again. There was another pile of something in the field. Then another. She sat upright. The next pile in the field, she thought, made what looked like the outline of an animal under the light of the moon. Then another. She whipped her head behind her, staring at it as they went by.

"You okay? What is it?" Garrett said, bringing the car to a slower pace.

"Stop the car!" Laura said.

Angela and Jerry woke in the backseat. Jerry leaned forward.

"What's going on? Are we there?" Jerry said, putting on his glasses.

Garrett stopped the car. He checked behind them for headlights, realizing, for now, they were the only car out and about tonight.

We shouldn't get out of this car.

"Did you see that? Did you see all of them?" Laura said as she shut the car door and stood on the shoulder of the interstate.

Garrett went to the back of the car, opened the trunk, and grabbed a black flashlight. He turned it on, then walked over to where Laura stood. Angela and Jerry both got out of the car slowly.

"What is it, Garrett?" Angela said, rubbing her shoulders as if she had just stepped outside in the dead of winter.

The four of them stood together, and Garrett raised the flashlight, powerful enough to illuminate a small portion of the field.

The carcasses of at least fifty half-eaten cows, deer, horses and dogs lay in the field. Those things had been here recently. Laura grabbed onto Garrett's arm as the four of them stared blankly into the field. Garrett's palms started to sweat.

And somewhere, not too far away, they were picking up their scent. They were coming.

Garrett, Laura, Angela, and Jerry stood there in silence. And they were being hunted.

The eyes glowing in the closet seem to disappear with the sunrise. But at night? At night, everything changes.

CHAPTER 41

Downtown, people were arriving at the LBD building in droves. Families, people all alone, and people with newborns were all standing at the door, checking in, answering the questions from the National Guard, and people wearing name tags.

A woman with a clipboard, who liked she hadn't slept in about a week, asked everyone the same questions.

"Name?"

"Address?"

"How many in your party?"

"How long do you plan to stay?"

Then, like going to the doctor for a checkup, everyone was lined up one by one, and their temperature was taken. If anyone had a fever, they were turned away. The next group of people would come up to her, the same questions were asked, and then, finally, they would hold the thermometer up to their foreheads like a radar gun. This had gone on for two days now.

There were three entrances to this place, each entrance with a single door, large and white and old looking. A small rectangular window sat solitarily on each heavy door in the upper right-hand corner, making its way almost halfway down the door. All three entrances were heavily guarded by the National Guard, with someone asking the same questions and taking temperatures over and over. It had filled up more rapidly than they had expected, and it wasn't long before they realized they would be over capacity.

The two ladies on the west side of the building could see each other, giving each other glances of uncertainty, knowing that soon they would have to turn people away, knowing the chaos it would cause. Not only that, they had to be the ones to look the elderly or small children in the eyes and give them the bad news.

No more room at the inn.

On the inside, each family was led to a large open room, divided between billowing white curtains. Inside of each curtain was a small rug and two or three cots placed horizontally. The cots, which were a drab green color, were old and stunk. They were never meant to hold more than one person, but here, people did what they had to do. Children slept with their parents, and depending on how many were in your party, a cot might be given to another family who needed it.

There were showers in a concrete room down the hall, an open room with three shower heads that hung on the wall like a high school locker room. Each family was given a shower schedule to ensure that families could shower as one, preventing any embarrassment if times overlapped.

Across from the showers, to the left and down the hall, stood the makeshift cafeteria. There were rows of white tables with stacked boxes of condiments with perforated cardboard edges. Bottles of water and cans of soft drinks set atop them in perfect rows. Families would be called every ten minutes in the morning, afternoon, and evening to eat their breakfast, lunch, and dinner as a group.

Lights went out at eleven pm and were turned back on at seven am. If anyone had small children that cried, everyone else had to deal with it. A baby crying in the night was the risk one took coming here to stay in a large group to be safe. Most people would agree that this was a risk worth taking, but some families had packed up and left after the second night, not being able to handle it. No one was forced to stay.

For the most part, everyone was genuinely happy to be here, and they felt safe and comforted by the fact that the National Guard kept a close watch outside. With hot and cold running water, decent food served three times a day, and a bed to sleep in, most found it very accommodating here. They were grateful for a government providing such care as this, allowing everyone to be with their families safely tucked in to the large, old building.

One of the ladies who worked outside was writing something down on her clipboard when her walkie-talkie beeped, then clicked with static.

"Anna, it's Tyson," the voice said.

Anna leaned her head to her shoulder, where the radio was clipped to her shirt. "Go ahead, Tyson."

"Yeah, we are almost there. Right now sitting about eighty percent capacity," Tyson said through some static.

"Copy. Let me know when I need to start turning them away," Anna said, then looked back down at her clipboard. She lifted a paper, then studied something underneath.

"Copy that," he said back to her.

CHAPTER 42

In a two-bedroom house located in the middle of nowhere, just outside Atlanta, Georgia, Tom Prather was trying to reach anyone on his HAM radio. Tom was a quiet man who mostly kept to himself, a shy single thirty-six-year-old man with no family.

In high school, his obsession had been electronics and radio, and he had joined the after-school program known as "ARC" (Amateur Radio Club), learning the ins and outs of operating high-frequency radio equipment. It was here, after school, where he learned to communicate over the waves to great distances. He had communicated with people from all across the globe, his longest transmission reaching just over three thousand miles. For years, he had studied books on the subject, spending most of his weekends at the local library while watching videos and documentaries at home.

Tom's story actually started about two weeks ago when he was picking up jumbled static on his end of the radio. He had been sitting at his old and dusty wooden desk, littered with books and magazines on international radio techniques, studying how to strengthen the signal on his radio.

A slight buzz, then a few crackles and pops, made its way through Tom's receiver. He looked up slowly from his book, frowned, then turned back to the book. He turned a page, adjusted his glasses, and yawned. Another crackle came through the small speaker. Tom sat up, bringing his feet to the floor. He sat the book down on the desk.

A noise that sounded like an airplane coming through the tiny speaker made him jump. He adjusted a few knobs on the machine, then jiggled the antennae.

A quiet, faint voice came through. "…hear me? Hello?" the voice said, sounding close but distant at the same time. Tom adjusted the knobs again as more static came through. He listened closely, the voice coming through again, this time even softer. The voice was calm, but there were undertones of panic that Tom picked up on. "…to…them. Do not trust…" the voice said, then more static. Tom stood up, turning around, unsure why he felt like someone was in the room with him.

More static and buzzing came through the speakers.

Tom grabbed a headset from the desk and fumbled it in his hands, almost dropping it on the floor. He put it on, then pushed a few buttons on the machine.

"Hello, are you there? This is Tom Prather from Atlanta, Georgia. Is someone there? I'm getting a lot of QRM during your last transmission," Tom said, sounding professional. He continued, "What is your QTH?" he said, realizing someone might not understand what that meant. "What is your location?" he said into his headset. He sat down at his desk.

More static came through. Then a long silence. Tom waited a few minutes, then took off his headset, placing it down on the table. He sat, staring at the radio. He picked up the book and began reading. After the turn of a few pages, he opened his notebook and started writing some notes. He looked back at the radio with a dumb look of anticipation painted on his face. He closed the book, then stood. He reached into the right pocket of his gray, worn jacket. He pulled out a pack of cigarettes, smacking them in his hand. Then, in his left pocket, he pulled out a small, yellow lighter. He held them up together, placed them in his right hand, then went out the front door for a smoke. Tom stood there, listening to the silence. He held his hand up to block the wind, then lit the cigarette. A plume of smoke floated in the air. Inside, the radio buzzed. More static came through.

"Don't go anywhere. Stay inside. If you are out there, if you can hear me, don't trust them. This is my final transmission. They're here."

CHAPTER 43

Jerry helped Angela back in the car, while Garrett did the same for Laura up front. It was raining now, and the temperature had dropped to an unusual cool. The sprinkle felt good to Garrett as he looked up, letting his face get a refreshing shower as Laura sat down in the passenger seat. Garrett made his way to the driver's side, hopped in, and started the ignition.

"We should be there in ten minutes or so," Garrett said to everyone as they drove off. He thought about one of those celebrity home tours in Los Angeles and Hollywood and laughed.

"If you look to your left, you will see the house belonging to the infamous so and so."

He drove on.

"I, for one, am ready to get out of this car for the night," Mrs. Bradley said. "I've had enough excitement for one day."

Everyone heard her, but no one acknowledged the statement. Fatigue, worry, and uncertainty had taken its toll.

"I just hope they have something somewhat comfortable to sleep on," Angela scoffed.

"Honey, we're not going to the Ritz Carlton," Jerry said, giving her a friendly glance.

Garrett looked in the rearview mirror and smiled. Laura was looking out the window, smiling but distant. She was still worried about her family, and her phone was still displaying the dreaded "No Service" message.

From this point, lights from downtown could be seen over the hill in front of them and through the trees on their left. They were getting close. Garrett's heart rate was elevated, and he noticed he was paying more attention to everything around him. Just ahead, the road snaked right, then eventually would curve around to the left again, just before he would exit for downtown.

Up ahead, there was something white in the road. To Garrett, it looked like someone had placed two sandbags up against the wall on the shoulder of the interstate. He couldn't see what it was through the windshield wipers and steady rain.

"What is that?" Garrett said.

"Slow down. It looks like a woman pushing a stroller," Laura said, moving her head to see.

Garrett gently lifted his foot, bringing the car to a slow pace. The four of them were trying to make out exactly what it was they were looking at. The rain had started to beat down harder, making it that much more difficult for the image to form into a discernible picture. Garrett pulled up to the edge of the road, his car halfway on the right shoulder. His tires buzzed and shook as he ran over the rumble strip. They stared as the woman pushed the stroller slowly. She looked straight ahead and kept walking.

Garrett put his car in park but kept it running. He opened the door.

"Hey! Are you okay?" he yelled, half out of his car, half standing in the right lane of the highway.

The woman stopped, then turned to face them. Her face looked ghost white. Her hair, dark and wet, hung freely in front of her face and on her shoulders. She kept one hand on the stroller and put one hand over her eyes, blocking out the headlights on Garrett's car.

"I'm trying to get to my mother," she said without expression. "I'm just trying to get us there. Me and my daughter."

With that, Jerry opened the car door.

"Jerry, don't," Angela said and grabbed him by the arm. "We don't know who she is. We don't know if we can trust her. Garrett, please. Keep going."

"Honey, she needs help, and she has a baby. We can't just leave her out here," Jerry said back to his wife.

He stood, then got out and shut the door. Angela was scared and did nothing to try to hide the look on her face.

"Garrett, be careful. We don't know if that's a…*you know.*" Laura said. Her voice was shaky and cold.

Garrett looked at her and started to say something, but didn't. He nodded, then shut the car door. The two

Bradley men walked toward the woman at a snail's pace, almost seeming to tip-toe.

"Where did you come from?" Garrett said, wiping some rain out of his eyes.

"I'm from Leddington, but my mother is on the north side of downtown. In Halton Heights," she said.

They made their way closer to her. Garrett, for the second time since he got out of the car, felt the cool of the gun against his back. It gave him more confidence than he would usually have in a situation like this. But then, had he ever been in a situation like this? Walking up to some strange woman on the highway, in the dark, in the rain? No, he couldn't say he had ever been placed in such a position as this before.

The night is terrifying.

"We can give you a ride," Garrett said. They were close now. Within a few feet. He noticed the stroller looked like one straight out of the 1980s. This caused him to be more hesitant, and he crinkled his face.

"That would be nice," she said, then messed with something in the stroller, making a movement as if she were petting a sleeping cat or dog.

"Let us help you," Jerry said, moving closer to her. "I can grab the baby," he said, smiling. "It's okay. We are here to help."

He walked up to the woman and held out his arms. He looked in the stroller, realizing there was nothing in it but a blanket. Jerry looked up at her, confused.

"Garrett!" Jerry said, his eyes wide and frightened. He was struck in the face by the woman, whose white skin slowly started transforming into a horrible color of green. Jerry flew backward in the air and landed in the ditch close to their car. Laura and Angela screamed.

Garrett reached for the gun at his back, but it grabbed him before he could get it out. It went for Garrett's throat, but he was able to land a punch to its face. It picked Garrett up and threw him like a rag doll. It turned toward the car, the yellow eyes a shade of neon in the beam of the headlights.

In two massive leaps, it was now on top of Jerry, standing over him. It smiled. The claw, sharp and glistening in the rain, was extended outward. It made one downward strike, and Jerry rolled out of the way. It struck the side of his face, leaving a scratch. Blood rose to the surface, his cheek becoming red and swollen, but it was a scratch not even deep enough to require stitches.

The thing let out a high pitch hiss, seeming annoyed now. The claw was raised in the air, this time fueled with rage and hate. The claw began its descent, the forward motion aiming to plunge deep into Jerry's chest. Laura and Angela screamed inside the car but were too in shock to move. They watched everything around them in slow motion. The hand came down as a deafening sound echoed in the air. The thing dropped, landing right next to Jerry. He could smell it. And there was Garrett, standing in the rain, pointing the gun in their direction. The gun was still smoking.

CHAPTER 44

Angela and Laura opened the car doors, then slammed them shut, running to Jerry. The rain, which had picked up when Garrett killed the thing, now slowed to less than a drizzle.

Jerry stood up, dusted himself off, then held his hand to his right cheek. There was a small dab of blood on his finger. His cheek stung, and he wiped it with his sleeve. He exhaled, realizing how lucky he had been to walk away with a small scratch. Angela grabbed him and started to cry.

"I'm fine. I'm okay, dear," he said, smiling.

"Thank God. I thought I was going to lose you," Angela said, hugging him now.

Garrett walked over to them, and Laura ran to him and grabbed him. The thing stared blankly up at the sky, the yellow eyes lifeless. Laura bent down and looked at it. She had never seen one up close. The smell made her think about tenth-grade biology when she had reluctantly dissected a baby pig in Mr. Harrison's class. She looked away in disgust.

Garrett sniffed, wiping a mix of sweat and rain out of his face. "This is a good example of why we need to stay together," he said. "You alright, dad?"

"Yes, I'm fine," Jerry said. "No more hitchhikers, though," he said and smiled.

"I have a first aid kit in the trunk. I think there's some bandages and gauze in there," Garrett said, walking toward the back of his car. The trunk opened with a click, and Garrett grabbed the white box with a red cross on it.

"Here you go," he said, and handed it to his dad. Angela took it from Jerry, opened it, and started rifling through its contents. She grabbed two bandages and a white cloth and held it up to his face. Garrett walked back over to the creature. The smell hit him again. He knelt down in a catcher's stance. Laura stood beside him.

"What is it?" she said, noticing the concern on Garrett's face.

"I've been up close and personal with these things a few times now." He paused, studying its face. "A few times too many. This is the first one that spoke…normally. No broken English, no weird dialect. Just normal English."

"What does that mean?" Laura said, kneeling down beside him. "Are you saying they are…changing?"

"I don't know. But if they are, we are going to have a hell of a time with these things," he said, then glanced back at his parents. Angela had placed two bandages on her husband's face. "We're not going to be able to tell the difference between people and.." he motioned toward the thing.

"Maybe we should get going, Garrett," Jerry said as he and Angela walked over to where Garrett and Laura were kneeling. "There might be more close by."

Garrett rose slowly. "Yeah," he said, still looking down at the thing. "Yeah, I think you're right."

The four of them got back into the car, and Garrett started it. He looked in the side mirror, then slowly pulled back onto the interstate.

"That one was different," Garrett said out loud. He wasn't necessarily talking to anyone in particular as much as he was just thinking out loud. "I think these things are changing. I think they are learning how to…act like us or something."

"Oh my God," Angela said from the back seat. "Garrett, we should go home. I'm scared."

"Honey, it'll be fine," Jerry said to her. "We've come this far, and we're sticking to the plan."

For the first time, Garrett was scared, too. Of course, he wouldn't show this on the outside, but inside he was the frightened child that was too scared to ride roller coasters until he was in his teens. The one that begged his parents to leave a light on in the hall at bedtime. And here he was now, trying to protect them. He wished this nightmare would end.

"Mom, we will be fine. We will stay together, surrounded by other people who are trying to do the same thing we are. Just trying to stay safe with our families. We will be just fine, but we have to stick together in there," Garrett said, looking out the windshield.

He brought the car to the exit that would lead them to the LBD building. The lights off to the left were getting brighter, illuminating the sky, mixing with the drizzle and fog that had crept in.

Garrett brought the car through a couple of right turns, followed by a left, then another. There were signs on the road here, directing traffic. Finally, he came upon a row of brown National Guard Humvees. There were two men standing here in uniform. Garrett pulled his car up, bringing it to a slow stop, then rolled down his window.

"How can I help you?" The man, dressed in camouflage, holding some type of automatic weapon, asked.

"Hey there. We are trying to get to the LBD building, for the…uhh…."

Laura leaned over and helped out, "Safe haven."

Garrett looked over at her and nodded.

"Yeah, for the safe haven," Garrett said, looking around. He was amazed at the number of people and vehicles that had been deployed. He had underestimated the scale of this.

"Okay," the man said, then pointed down the street. "You're going to make your first right where that orange sign is. Then your first left. That'll take you straight there. But you might want to hurry, last word we received was that they were almost over capacity."

"Oh, wow. Great, thanks. Stay safe out here," Garrett said, then rolled up the window. The man didn't acknowledge his last statement and waved them on.

Garrett drove on, hoping they still had room for a party of four.

CHAPTER 45

They pulled up to the gate, slowly being directed where to go by multiple men in matching uniforms. Their car, rolling and stopping frequently, was third in line to be parked, making their way to another abandoned lot that had been demolished the year before. Garrett followed the cars in front of him. The red of the taillights flashed in his face and showed his exhaustion. Another man holding the same type of rifle as the ones before him waved him on. Garrett turned right into the abandoned lot and was then directed to park next to the car in front of him. He saw an older woman in the passenger seat and a woman he guessed to be about his age driving. Garrett took the key out of the ignition, turning on the interior light of his car. He turned around to face his parents and Laura.

"We stay together. No matter what. That's all we need to remember right now," Garrett said, sounding stern. Laura and his parents agreed.

Garrett got out of the car, looking around. He saw a long line of people waiting to get in. There were those same men, with their long assault rifles, walking around, directing people where to go. The sounds of radios were going off with static, beeps, and clicks. The sound of Humvees and other vehicles reverberated off the buildings and down the alley. It seemed like organized chaos.

Garrett opened the trunk and got everyone's bags out, handing it to them one by one. He started to give the bag he had packed for his parents to Jerry.

"Need me to carry this, pops?"

"I'm old, but I'm not dead," Jerry said, then took the bag from Garrett. They both laughed.

"Okay, just trying to help, old man," Garrett said, winking at Laura. She smiled while Angela laughed.

He didn't ask Laura; he just threw her bag on his right shoulder, then threw his bag over his left, closing the trunk.

"Let me get it," Laura said.

"No, it's okay. I've got it," Garrett said. Laura kissed his cheek.

"Well, let's go get in line, I guess," Garrett said. He started walking, then stopped. "Stick together."

They went through an open gate at the entrance of the abandoned lot where they parked. They noticed people getting their temperatures checked and answering questions from a lady holding a clipboard. Jerry stopped, put a hand over his face to block out the light coming from the roof, and noticed men and women in uniform pacing on top of the LBD building and the building behind it. It was the first time Jerry realized the magnitude of what was happening here.

"Keep moving!" A voice was yelling near them. Jerry flinched, then realized the man was talking to him.

"Come on, Jerry," Angela said, and waved him toward them. They had moved about ten feet ahead of him.

They walked through a sloshy space of little brown and white rocks, stepping over puddles where the gravel had retained some water. They entered through another gate, silver, and chain-linked, that looked like it had been put up in a hurry over the last few days. There was a white sign with an arrow that pointed to the line. They stepped that way and fell in behind a family of a mom, dad, and two small girls. The youngest girl, holding a stuffed unicorn in one hand and her dad's hand in the other, turned and looked at Laura. Laura waved and smiled. The little girl did the same back to her.

A man stood next to the woman holding the clipboard, both of them talking into the radios on their shoulders. She pointed in the direction of Garrett. The man looked toward Garrett, then said something else into his radio. He pointed again in Garrett's direction, then turned to say something to the woman with the clipboard. Garrett tried to read their lips but couldn't. He looked at Laura, trying to see if she could make out the panic on his face. He must have hid it well because she smiled and put her head on his shoulder.

The man nodded, then walked toward Garrett.

Please don't turn us away. God, please don't turn us away, Garrett thought to himself. He let out a sigh, trying to slow his heart rate. The man made eye contact with him as he walked right for him. Garrett closed his eyes, a tactic he learned when he was a kid. *If I can't see them, they can't see me.* The man walked past Garrett, approaching the three people behind him. He turned to listen to the conversation.

"I'm sorry. We will have to stop right here for the night. You can try again tomorrow," he said.

Garrett felt a mix of relief and guilt, trying not to look at the families being turned away. The last thing he could stomach today would be to see a child having to go home or wherever they would go tonight, knowing he took their spot.

Sorry, but I'm scared too. The night is terrifying.

The line started to move.

CHAPTER 46

Garrett, Laura, Angela, and Jerry were up next. The family with the two small girls were ahead of them, answering questions. The woman with the clipboard looked mad or exhausted, but in all the madness, it could have very well been both.

The temperatures and questions were scanned and answered satisfactorily, and the family made their way inside. Garrett stepped up, holding Laura's hand.

The lady with the clipboard was writing something down. She looked up at Garrett, and he noticed the puffiness under her eyes. Dark half-circles underneath amplified the bloodshot where her eyes had once been white. She was exhausted.

"How many are in your party?" she said, holding the pen, ready to write his responses down.

"There are four of us," Garrett said, looking back at his parents. Laura stood silently, holding his hand.

"Names?" she said, without looking up.

They went one by one.

"Garrett Bradley."

"Laura Wright."

"Angela Bradley."

"Jerry Bradley."

The lady was still writing when she asked a third question. "Address?"

Garrett decided to just give his address. "2133 Madden Court. Burnley, Michigan."

The tip of her tongue was sticking out of her mouth as she kept writing. She waved her hand, flinging it in the air like she had a cramp. She continued. "How long do you intend to stay?"

Garrett looked at Laura, then at his parents. "I guess we will stay the duration of the quarantine." He paused, looking down at the ground. He raised it as if a thought had just come to mind. "Are we free to come and go as we please?"

"You are free to go anytime. But if you leave, you will be placed at the back of the line again. So, I would not recommend that if you want to keep your place."

She grabbed the thermometer, clipped to her side, and held it up. She scanned Garrett, Laura, and the Bradley couple, everyone's temperature 98.6 or below, as indicated by the green light that flashed.

I wonder what happens if it flashes red, Garrett thought to himself.

A man in uniform stepped forward. "You four with me," he said, motioning them toward him. "Here's the deal. You're going to go inside. You are going to wait at the first door. Someone will meet you there and lead you to where you are going to stay for the duration of your time here. He or she will give you your schedule, such as shower times and meals. Do you understand?"

Garrett and Laura nodded, while Angela and Jerry struggled to hear from behind. They saw Garrett and Laura nod, trusting they'd be filled in later. They nodded.

The man held an ID up to the door, and it buzzed, then opened. It was a heavy door, and it opened with a click that was louder than expected. The four of them stepped inside and the door shut with an echo that made Angela jump.

A woman dressed in white approached them. "Hello, I'm Jane," she said, smiling at them. She handed Garrett a piece of paper.

"I'm Garrett. This is my girlfriend, Laura. And my parents, Jerry and Angela," Garrett said, introducing everyone to her.

She smiled, then led them through another set of doors. "This paper has your schedule on it. We tried to spread it out as much as possible so that there's not a lot of chaos trying to eat meals or take showers. When you get to your quarters, you will see a basket with bars of soap, shampoo, and a toothbrush and toothpaste if you did not think of bringing any toiletries. Lights are out at eleven pm, and they will come back on at seven am. Other than that, everything should be self-explanatory."

"How many people are here?" Jerry asked.

"Tonight, we have right at four thousand. But everyone is working hard to make more space. We would love to have as many people here as possible," she said as she kept walking.

"Wow!" Jerry said, looking at Angela. Everyone else was wide-eyed at the idea of four thousand people fitting in this building. Jerry had a hard time wrapping his mind around it.

She made a right down the hall, through another set of double doors, and the sound of people talking grew louder. It reminded Garrett of the sound of a gymnasium filled with people on Friday nights when he was in high school and would go to basketball games with his buddies.

She turned again, this time making a left, through one more set of doors. The light was bright, but the first thing Garrett noticed was the huge white curtains that hung from the rafters in the ceiling. It looked like an old gymnasium that had been set up for the homeless. He could hear kids playing and laughing, and somewhere, not too far off, he heard a baby screaming.

Garrett turned and looked at his dad. "We'll see how well you sleep tonight, pops."

Jerry gave him a sarcastic smile.

Jane led them to their quarters that had two cots- both an olive-green color, with white and brown sheets and blankets folded neatly on them. They weren't big, but they would be able to fit two people on them fairly easily.

"Any questions?" Jane said as they started putting their bags down on the cots.

"No, I think we're good. We appreciate your help," Garrett said.

"Well, if you need anything, anything at all, just find me. Again, my name is Jane." She smiled, then walked away.

Garrett noticed Laura looking at the bed. "I can sleep on the floor. It's fine. I can fall asleep anywhere," he said to her.

"Yeah, like his father," Angela said, laughing. She grabbed the basket from the floor and placed it on the cot.

"No, it's fine. Actually, I would feel more comfortable having you close to me tonight," Laura said.

Garrett smiled, feeling like he wanted to grab her and kiss her right here. His parents were watching, and he felt like a teenager again. He pulled her in close and hugged her. She fell into him. She needed that hug more than anything right now. She was sure she was falling in love with him. She wanted to get out of this mess and pursue him. She thought about the future.

Jerry took the paper out of Garrett's hand that was at the lower part of Laura's back.

"Oh, good. Looks like we get to shower in the morning. I can't start my day without one," Jerry said.

Garrett thought about it for a minute, then leaned in and kissed Laura. Her eyes closed, and she regretted being stuck in this building for the next ten days or so.

Jerry unzipped his bag and started going through it.

Down the hall, Jane was making her way back to the next family that needed in. It was a middle-aged man and his son. Jane approached them, smiling. The father and son duo smiled back with backpacks draped over their shoulders.

"Hello, I'm Jane," she said. "Glad you could be here with us tonight."

Everyone had been too busy looking around. Their guard had let up just long enough not to notice.

There was something about Jane. Wasn't there?

She closed the door behind them, and her yellow eyes reflected off the glass window on the door. It echoed loudly in the empty hall.

They evolved quickly. They had outsmarted humanity almost from the very beginning. They had used one of man's greatest inventions and were now destroying them with it. Social media was a powerful tool, and they had used it to herd people here like sheep.

"Right this way," Jan said, then led them down the hall with the rest of them.

CHAPTER 47

Two days later, a small TV that hung in the corner of an empty waiting room at a local doctor's office was getting ready to be shut off by the administrative assistant. Her instructions had been to work until today, then begin her quarantine that would last for ten more days. The TV, at a low, muffled volume, was playing an afternoon talk show. The woman, who was overweight and had red hair, reached up to turn it off. As she did so, the talk show was interrupted by breaking news and went to a local news feed. She stepped back and watched.

It was downtown, and it looked like people were running away from something. She thought she heard gunfire in the background.

"What you are seeing is a live look downtown, where we have just learned of mass casualties at the LBD building. This was one of the government held safe havens. Now, we are not aware of the details, but Ben Shellin is live at the site. Ben?"

"That's right, Bob. People are running in every direction. It is mass chaos at the site right now. Police seem to be struggling to maintain order. Let's see if we can get a word with someone now." He walked over, dodging a few people. *"Excuse me, sir? Sir! Sir, can you tell me what has happened here?"*

"Don't come down here! Stay at home with your loved ones! I was one of the lucky ones and was able to get my girlfriend and parents out of here alive. We are getting out of here!"

The camera followed them as they got into a black Toyota Camry and drove off.